The Final Martyrs

Books By Shusaku Endo
Available From New Directions

Deep River
The Final Martyrs
Five By Endo
The Girl I Left Behind
The Samurai
The Sea and Poison
Stained Glass Elegies

The Final Martyrs

Shusaku Endo

Introduction by Caryl Phillips
Afterword by the Author
Translated by Van C. Gessel

 A NEW DIRECTIONS BOOK

Translated from the Japanese: The Final Martyrs (*Saigo no junkyōsha*, 1959);
Shadows (*Kagebōshi*, 1968); A Fifty-year-old Man (*Gojussai no otoko*, 1973); Adieu
(*A Dyū*, 1978); Heading Home (*Kaerinan*, 1979); Japanese in Warsaw (*Warushawa
no Nipponjin*, 1979); Life (*Jinsei*, 1981); A Sixty-year-old Man (*Rokujassai no otoko*,
1983); The Last Supper (*Saigo no bansan*, 1984); A Woman called Shizu (*Shizu to iu
hito*, 1985); The Box (*Hako*, 1985).

Manufactured in the United States of America
Cover design by Ann Weinstock
New Directions Books are printed on acid-free paper.
First published clothbound by New Directions in 1994
Published as a New Directions Paperbook (NDP1132) in 2009
Published by arrangement with Peter Owen Publishers, London

Library of Congress Cataloging-in-Publication Data

Endo, Shusaku, 1923–1996.
　[Short stories. English. Selections]
The final martyrs / introduction by Caryl Phillips ; afterword by the Author ;
translated by Van C. Gessel.
　p. cm.
"First published clothbound by New Directions in 1994."
ISBN 978-0-8112-1811-5
1. Endo, Shusaku, 1923-1996–Translations into English. I. Gessel, Van C. II. Title.
PL849.N4A6 2008
895.6'35—dc22

2008041983

New Directions Books are published for James Laughlin
by New Directions Publishing Corporation
80 Eighth Avenue, New York, NY 10011

Contents

Introduction by Caryl Phillips

Shusaku Endo's collection of short stories *The Final Martyrs* was first published in English in 1993. These eleven stories were actually written between 1959 and 1985, and therefore represent almost the full breadth of Endo's distinguished career as a writer. Inevitably, the stories rehearse some of the themes that appear, more fully fleshed out, in his major novels, and in Endo's brief but illuminating afterword, the author admits to using the short story form as a kind of literary micro-laboratory where he is able to experiment freely.

> When . . . characters begin to move, I write a short story about them in a different locale. This allows me to breathe a fuller life into them. As a result, I can only assume that the characters who appear in the short stories collected here must be living in some form or other in the longer works that I am composing even now.

Endo also incorporates incidents from his own life into his short stories, and he draws upon these autobiographical details in order to trigger his imagination, a technique that he creatively employs in much of his longer fiction. As the stories develop (and they are usefully collected chronologically) we see the author making himself increasingly visible, a narrative strategy that required considerable courage coming, as he did, from a country and a culture which cherishes discretion.

Shusaku Endo was born in Tokyo in 1923. He spent part of his childhood in Japanese-occupied Manchuria, but when he was ten years old his parents divorced and he returned with his mother to her hometown, Kobe. In 1935, he was baptized as a Catholic, at a time when fewer than one percent of the Japanese population was Christian. Almost inevitably, during this particularly nationalistic period of Japanese history, Endo was bullied for his faith. This oppression served to not only deepen his belief, but it seems to have also bestowed upon him a profound understanding of what it means to be an outsider. After the Second World War, Endo was the first Japanese student to study abroad. He traveled to France, where he studied Catholic Literature at the University of Lyon, and it was in France that he began to experience the existential difficulties of being looked upon, and treated, as a foreigner. Endo returned to Japan in 1953 and embarked upon a literary career that soon saw him recognized as a novelist of the first-rank, but he also wrote short stories, essays and was involved in theatre and television.

Silence (1966) is regarded by most critics as his masterpiece. In this novel, he recounts the story of a Portuguese missionary in early seventeenth-century Japan who publicly apostatizes, but inwardly still maintains some vestige of faith. The missionary hopes that his weakness and betrayal might eventually be forgiven, but his inner turmoil remains profound. The title story of *The Final Martyrs* is the earliest piece in this collection, and it recalls the communal life of a group of seventeenth-century Nagasaki Christians who, across the years, secretly hold on to their faith despite generations of persecution. At the heart of the story is a very familiar Endo character, a "weak" Christian who oscillates between his fear of torture and his inability to totally abandon Jesus Christ. A variation on this theme can be found in the story "A Sixty-year-old Man," in which a writer, who is clearly based on the author, is tempted by his lust for young girls even as he rehearses in his mind a revision of a book based on the life of Christ. As with "The Final Martyrs" it is clear that the narrative seeds that are sown here will eventually flower in a novel, in this case, *Scandal* (1986).

The authorial, "experimental," hand feels uncomfortably heavy in some of these stories. "Japanese in Warsaw," in which the author satirizes a self-serving group of Japanese male tourists, who seem interested in little more than the possibility of sex with Polish women, ends with a neat twist of plot that one senses is somewhat pre-ordained by the author. The same might be said of the neat symbolism of "A Fifty-year-old Man," but these are minor quibbles for Endo himself is clear about the degree of "rehearsal" occurring in his short stories. However, even when a story seems a little too constructed, Endo always manages to portray characters of great complexity who are battling their inner demons in a manner which draws us to them irrespective of what we may think of their morality. Shimizu, the tour guide in "Japanese in Warsaw," is one such individual, a man who is facilitating the licentious behavior of these tourists, but who understands that he must perform a role if he is going to survive the situation that has been thrust upon him.

> *Over the year he had been guiding Japanese tourists for the travel company, Shimizu had gradually determined that he would turn himself into a sort of machine. A machine that would welcome them at the airport, and see them off at the airport ... A machine that would take them to taverns and snack-bars where they could meet women. A machine that would listen as they ridiculed the poverty of Poland. A machine that would never let its own thoughts or feelings show on its face.*

This passage leads us closer to an understanding of the great theme at the heart of Endo's work, and one which often made his Japanese public uncomfortable. How do we, as modern people, navigate a world which wishes to endorse and reward a conformist, unilateral approach to matters of culture and faith, when travel and migration have brought us face to face with other ways of living and being in the world? Many of Endo's characters fall mute or, like Shimizu, put on a mask. Endo's people are quiet individuals behind whose often implacable façade an internal battle is raging, one which may well eventually tear them apart. Time does not appear to heal any wounds, for there is a wonderful chronological sweep to a great number of Endo's stories in which the true horror of an event that took place decades ago can be suddenly pulled into focus by the smallest of contemporary incidents.

In his own life, Endo grappled with the notion of a troubled past that he might never be able to fully resolve and which he gradually came to accept would probably haunt him for the remainder of his days. In this collection of stories, he constantly fixes, and refixes, his gaze on the lonely figure of a young boy living with his mother in Japanese-occupied Manchuria, and enduring a hostile climate, yet who remains unclear as to why his mother wishes him to take on a faith that places him in opposition to the vast majority of Japanese people. It is a faith that the young boy understands does not sit well with his culture, but the boy perseveres. And then later, he voluntarily takes a deliberate step into a further kind of exile by becoming a Japanese student abroad. In 1901, the Japanese writer Natsume Soseki in "Letter from London" gave us some insight into what such a temporary exile might feel like, describing himself as appearing to European eyes to be a "strangely complexioned Tom Thumb." He continued: "When I was in Japan I knew I was not particularly white but regarded myself as being close to a regular human color, but in this country I have finally realized that I am three leagues away from a human color—a yellow person who saunters amongst the crowds going to watch plays and shows . . ."

In Endo's story, "Adieu," which is set in the home of an elderly French couple in Lyon who are lodging a Japanese student, one can clearly feel Endo exploring this second aspect of his alienation, in one of his most subtle and moving stories. These same thematic concerns reappear in "A Summer in Rouen" (Part One of *Foreign Studies*), which looks closely at the relationship between a Japanese student and a French family, and the almost unbearable nervousness and high anxiety which consumes the poor student.

Shusaku Endo died in 1996, leaving an extraordinary body of work which speaks with both subtlety and eloquence to the situation of the outsider. His name was frequently mentioned as a candidate for the Nobel Prize for Literature, but this honor eluded him. Many critics have speculated that the supposedly pornographic nature of his novel, *Scandal* made some in Sweden uncomfortable, but what is undeniable is that Endo was a man unafraid to tackle the dark and truly problematic side of our warring impulses. On a recent visit to Tokyo, my Japanese publisher handed me a copy of an Endo novel that remains untranslated into English. The title of the book is *Nigger*, and it concerns a black man in seventeenth-century Japan. I was not surprised that the book had not been translated into English, but it seemed somehow appropriate that Shusaku Endo would have chosen to tackle this subject. As readers in English we remain extremely fortunate to have the majority of Endo's work available to us. Those who already know Endo's work will find much in this collection of short stories to remind them of the author at his best. For those new to Endo, *The Final Martyrs* probably represents an excellent place from which to start to familiarize oneself with one the great writers of the twentieth century.

New York, August 27, 2008

The Final Martyrs

The Final Martyrs

In the Uragami district not far from Nagasaki is a village called Nakano. Today it's a part of Hashiguchi-chō, but once it was a tiny community known simply as Nakano Village.

Early in the Meiji period, a man named Kisuke lived in this village. Physically he was as huge as an elephant, but his cowardice belied his size, and he was ineffectual no matter what task he was set to do. He tried with all his might to succeed, but whether he was planting rice paddies, or harvesting the plants, or helping out with roof-thatching in early spring at the orders of the village co-operative union, in the end his youthful co-workers, unable to watch his clumsiness any longer, would always end up lending him a hand.

'I hate working with you, Kisuke. We always have to fix things up after you've finished.' When his compatriots Kanzaburō and Zennosuke complained to him in this manner, Kisuke contracted his huge body as much as possible, and all he could do was bow his head deeply and say: 'Forgive me. Kanzaburō, please forgive me!'

Another problem was that, despite his youth, Kisuke was a hopeless sissy. He should have had no cause for fear, since his size and strength exceeded that of most young men his age. But let a single snake cross the road in front of him, and he would freeze in terror. Had some pranksters from the village draped a snake's corpse over the end of a pole and brought it to Kisuke, saying, 'Kisuke, this is for you!', his face would have paled like that of a little girl.

Once Kisuke, on his way home from working in the fields, was challenged to a fight by two drunken young men from a neighbouring village. The two trouble-makers had, of course, thrown down the gauntlet knowing full well that Kisuke was the infamous coward of Nakano village.

Kisuke retreated to the edge of the road and covered his trembling face with one hand. 'Please pardon me. Please forgive me.'

The two men, understandably disgusted with Kisuke for quivering like a baby when he was twice the size of a normal man, retorted: 'Hey, you call yourself a man? If you're a man, up with your fists. C'mon, your fists!'

Then they taunted him, coaxing him to prove he was a man by stripping down and showing them the evidence. Kisuke pleaded with them not to make him do that, but his cowering posture had the adverse effect of filling his opponents with a sadistic pleasure. 'Come on, strip down! So you won't, eh?'

For the sheer fun of it, they rubbed Kisuke's face into the ground as they might have tormented a puppy-dog.

The villagers of Nakano were legitimately irate when they learned how Kisuke had come stealing back into the village that night, stripped even of his loincloth and concealing his private parts. In Nakano village the proscribed Christian faith had been practised in secret over the years, unbeknown to the officials, and precisely because there was so much solidarity among the villagers, they could not forgive the fact that Kisuke had been taken for a fool by young men from another community. The youths of the village vowed they would never again speak to such a weakling, and the children, in their own callow way, began throwing horse dung and stones at the tumbledown shack where Kisuke and his mother lived.

Still, it made the villagers sad to see Kisuke set out for the fields each day with his hoe on his shoulder and his eyes lowered in misery. The elders from the co-operative began quoting Jesus' words to the young people: 'Whosoever shall smite thee on thy right cheek, turn to him the other also.' The residents of Nakano half grudgingly forgave Kisuke, who had become a laughing-stock in another village.

Because the villagers in Nakano in the Uragami district had sustained their belief in Christianity, in violation of the prohibition against the faith that the new Meiji government had inherited from the Tokugawa shogunate, their village organization was slightly different from those in other hamlets populated by Buddhist adherents. The Christian villages of Kyushu established various organizations based on age, which in today's terms would be described as a 'youth group', an 'adult group', a 'children's association' and a 'women's organization'. These groups together formed the religious league known as the 'co-operative union'. Names such as the 'Santa Maria Union' or the 'Jesus Union' were attached to each organization, and the union heads were elected to perform various duties. To assist the union heads, one, and sometimes several, service volunteers were put into place. Based on an entry in the Christian historical documents that reads, 'The number of union heads and service volunteers should be determined on the basis of location and circumstances', it appears that the numbers of these officials varied from village to village.

Kisuke belonged to the young people's organization in his village, but the level of his faith can be determined from the following anecdote.

In the spring of one year a beggar came to live on the outskirts of the village. But he was no ordinary beggar. He was a leper, and his fingers and toes were gnarled, all the hair had fallen from his head, and his eyes were half blinded. He had been driven from one village to the next before he finally arrived in Nakano, where he was fortunate enough to be able to lay himself down in an abandoned hut beside the banks of the river that flowed near the village.

Because the leaders of the co-operative were responsible not only for governing the village but for playing the role of priests who strengthened the faith of the villagers, they taught their followers how they should treat this beggar. They related how in olden days Jesus had stretched forth His hand to the lepers, and they ordered the union members to take turns caring for the suppliant. The villagers thereupon set up a schedule by which each would deliver rice balls and medicine every day to the riverside hut.

It was in early summer some two months later that Kisuke's turn came. This was an act of mercy that even a child could perform, and Kanzaburō and Zennosuke from his youth group merely told him: 'Kisuke, just like the chief said, he's a poor, unfortunate invalid, so be sure you take him some warm rice balls during the day and again at night.'

On his assigned day, as he set out to work in the fields, Kisuke had his mother prepare the medications and the rice balls as everyone had instructed him. That afternoon, he headed for the deserted riverbed. It was an early summer's day, warm enough to squeeze out a little perspiration, and when he stepped down into the riverbed, the stench of reeds rotted to their roots attacked his nose. The roof of the decaying hut peeked almost blackly from between the reeds. He could hear not a single sound; he wondered what the beggar was doing. It was so quiet all around him, he felt ill at ease.

When he arrived at the doorway, nervously clutching the bag containing the rice and medicines, the splintered door made an eerie sound as it creaked open. When fearfully he peered inside, the face of the beggar, with eye-sockets gaping like caverns and bereft of a nose, appeared before Kisuke.

'Uwaaah!'

Hurling the bag down, Kisuke fled from the hut, nearly stumbling as he made for the riverbed. The beggar had just grabbed on to the pillar and pulled himself to his feet, intending to go out and drink some of the stagnant water in the riverbed.

After he raced back to the village, Kisuke refused to return to the hut ever again, no matter how much his fellow-villagers entreated him. As always, in his childlike way he simply pleaded: 'Please forgive me. Please forgive me!'

The union heads and elder rulers of the village harshly chastened Kisuke for his lack of charity, citing the example of St Sebastian, who had held lepers in his arms to keep them warm. Absorbing the rebuke, Kisuke made one more attempt to deliver a package of rice balls in the evening, but no sooner had he left the village than he came running back. He clutched his hands together in entreaty: 'I'll do anything else you ask. But please don't make me do this!'

At that time one of the village rulers, a man named Taira no Kunitarō, who would later be martyred at the Sakura-chō prison in Nagasaki, remarked with a gloomy expression: 'One day Kisuke's cowardice may cause him to become like Judas, who betrayed our Saviour.'

In the fifth year of the Ansei era (1858), the Tokugawa shogunate abandoned its long tradition of isolationism and signed a trade agreement with the United States. The eighth article of that treaty stipulated that 'American citizens residing in Japan shall be allowed free exercise of their own religion, and will be allowed to erect places of worship near their dwellings.' This effectively did away with the use of the *fumie*. Similar treaties were signed with Britain, France, Russia and Holland the following year.

In 1859 the Parisian missionary, Father Girard,[1] who had been waiting for some time at Naha in Okinawa, entered Edo as a priest for the French Embassy in the capital. He was followed the next year by Revd Bernard Petitjean,[2] who landed at Nagasaki and erected a church in the Ōura hills to the south of Nagasaki with the help of Japanese carpenters. This was the original structure of the Ōura Church that was demolished by the atomic bomb.

The Japanese of the day, who called this church the 'French Temple', flocked curiously around to observe the construction of the chapel, but before long they stopped coming, owing perhaps to harassment from the government. Even though the treaty had permitted the practice of the Christian faith by foreigners, the ban on the religion among the Japanese con-

1. Prudence Séraphin Barthélemy Girard, a French missionary born in 1821, went to work in Japan in 1858. He died in 1867 in a fire that destroyed the church he built in Yokohama.
2. Father Petitjean (1829–84) reached Nagasaki in 1863, where he helped built the Ōura chapel. He died in Nagasaki and was buried in the chapel.

tinued. Both Father Petitjean and Father Laucaigne,[3] who reached Japan a year later, had heard while still in their native lands that some believers still secretly continued to follow the faith they had been taught when St Francis Xavier came to this island nation in the Far East. Once the chapel was built, the first mission they had to carry out was to locate these 'hidden' Christians.

But a month passed, then another month, and the chapel still had no visitors. The two priests frequently set out for Nagasaki and the environs of Uragami. Sometimes they would give sweets to children, at other times they would pretend to have fallen from a horse. But not a single Japanese came forward to confess in secret that he was a Christian.

The situation changed on the afternoon of 17 March 1865. That afternoon, Father Petitjean was kneeling at the altar in prayer. It was quiet that afternoon in the chapel. The door creaked faintly but, certain that this must be a police patrolman peeking in half in jest, he continued praying. Someone quietly approached him. When he turned round, a peasant woman dressed in a worker's smock stood stiff as a rod.

'The statue . . .?' She spoke softly. 'Where is the statue of Santa Maria?'

At her words Father Petitjean rose from the prayer altar. He spoke not a word, but his trembling finger indicated a two-foot statue of the Holy Mother positioned to the right of the altar.

'Ah, Santa Maria!' the woman cried. 'Oh my, how sweet the Holy Child is!'

This was the initial exchange between the first priest who had come to Japan after over two hundred years of exclusionary policies and the *kakure* Christians of Japan. The hidden Christians, while pretending on the surface to be followers of Buddhism, had secretly continued to intone their ancient Latin prayers and to live the teachings of the Church preached to them by their parents in Nagasaki and Uragami, as well as in

---

3. Joseph Marie Laucaigne (1838–85) came to Japan in 1863 and assisted Petitjean in his missionary work. He also worked in Nagasaki and Osaka. He took care of Petitjean during his final illness, then became fatally ill himself.

out-of-the-way villages facing the sea, and on islands in the harbour such as Gotō and Hirado.

In this way contact was established with the faithful, but the government had still not granted freedom of worship. To ward off persecution, Fathers Petitjean and Laucaigne decided to visit the villages and islands where the believers were hidden. They shaved off their curly locks and whiskers, donned wigs made of black-dyed fur from the hemp palm tree and put on peasant clothing. Under cover of darkness they climbed into a boat and travelled from village to village, guided by believers who led them along valley footpaths.

The government officials naturally were aware of the priests' movements. One of the magistrates of Nagasaki at the time, Governor Tokunaga of Iwami, had been tracking down Christians in the Uragami district, and in the summer of 1867 he gave orders to 170 constables to arrest any believers who had violated the prohibition on Christianity. On 15 July, just past midnight, Nakano village was raided. This was the beginning of the great suppression that came to be known as the 'fourth persecution at Uragami'.[4]

July is the month when typhoons hammer Kyushu. Heavy rains had fallen from morning on the fifteenth. By night the rains had been joined by wind.

Amidst the raging storm the village slept like the dead, but at that late hour constables carrying paper lanterns had already begun to surround the village of Nakano.

In a thatched-roof shed at the crossroads by the village shrine, three young men kept night watch, listening to the sound of the rain and the howling of the wind as they sipped their tea, unaware of what was happening outside. The faithful in Nakano called this shed the 'Francis Xavier Chapel'. It was a secret place where the villagers could hold their private meetings and offer up their prayers.

---

4. Uragami was first raided by authorities searching for *kakure* Christians in 1790, in 1842, and again in 1859. During this fourth raid, which lasted from 1867 to 1873, over a hundred were jailed, sixty of whom died from torture and exposure.

The three young night guards were Kanzaburō, Zennosuke, and Kisuke, who dozed in a corner of the room clutching the knees of his work clothes.

Casting an occasional glance towards Kisuke, Kanzaburō and Zennosuke were discussing whether they were prepared to die for their faith if, by chance, they should be subjected to the tortures of persecution.

'Well, I might be afraid. I might be afraid, but in that moment I know that the Lord Jesus would help me,' Kanzaburō declared defiantly. 'I'm determined to endure torture to the very end.'

'What about Kisuke?' Looking a bit uneasy, Zennosuke deflected the focus of the conversation. They glanced at their huge friend, who was sawing logs beneath the flickering light of the candle.

'He has a weakness for pain, after all, so I imagine he'd whimper in agony. Why, maybe he might even abandon the Lord Jesus and "topple".'

'Topple', of course, meant to forsake one's faith. They had known Kisuke since childhood, but as they thought of his usual cowardice and awkwardness, they had the distinct impression that he would be the first among the young people of the village to howl in torment. They remembered the words that the village elder, Kunitarō, had muttered with a dark expression: 'One day Kisuke's cowardice may cause him to become like Judas, who betrayed our Saviour.' He had uttered the warning as though he were a prophet.

'What time is it?' Kanzaburō asked.

'Must be about 2 a.m.'

Just then, mingling with the sounds of the wind and rain, they heard the piercing tone of a whistle. At that signal the constables who had been waiting on the outskirts of the city with lassos and clubs in hand stormed along the levee and into Nakano village. What followed were the sounds of doors being broken in, and the shouts of the constables. In later years Kanzaburō, who survived the whole ordeal, described the situation that night in the following words:

'Zennosuke escaped out the lattice door. Kisuke was caught

with one of the ropes. I put my hands behind my back, and told them to go ahead and tie me up. "Don't try to bewitch us!" they shouted, and they seemed very afraid of me and wouldn't come near. They threw a lasso round me and three of them tied me up tight. I couldn't breathe, and I passed out. They revived me by giving me water and smelling-salts. Then they dragged me off and stuck me in the village headman's rice granary.

'Some people had their heads cracked open and were covered with blood. Others were tightly bound up. By the time the sun had started to shine in the east, nearly a hundred had been arrested. Then they beat us on our backsides with whips and drove us out of the rice granary. The officers wore headbands tied behind their heads, and they waved their naked swords. We had to run lickety-split down to Nagasaki, where they put us in the prison at Sakura-chō.'

His manner of expression was crude, but it painted a vivid picture of the events of that night.

And so the fourth persecution at Uragami began. Once the inconsequential invalids and women and children were released from the Sakura-chō prison, thirty-eight men, including young men and their aged leaders, were stuffed into a narrow, stifling cell. Included in this group were Kanzaburō, Zennosuke and the face and large body of Kisuke, who, needless to say, was panic-stricken.

The next day several of the men were hauled before the court. Those who refused to 'topple' were submitted to a torture known as *dodoi*. Their arms and legs, throat and chest were bound with ropes, which were all knotted together in one spot behind their backs. Then they were hoisted up on to a cross, while officers who stood below struck them fiercely with poles and whips. They were lowered to the ground and water was poured over them. The ropes would absorb the water and constrict tightly, gnawing into the flesh of the captives. Those who remained in the cell heard cries like the dark yowls of wild creatures coming from the court, punctuated by taunts from the officers.

'Kisuke, be brave!'

Withstanding the cries of torment, Kanzaburō at once commanded and encouraged Kisuke, who sat to his side pale and clutching the bars of the cell.

'Pray to Santa Maria. To Santa Maria. . . .'

The others in the cell joined in a chorus of prayers for protection to the Holy Mother Mary, as though the idea had occurred to them only after Kanzaburō's remark. Amid the muffled, praying voices, Kisuke alone clung desperately to the bars, his pale lips quivering.

'Be brave, Kisuke!'

But suddenly, as if he had gone mad, Kisuke cried out in a loud voice. He was yelling to a warder standing outside the cell. 'Please forgive me! Please forgive me!'

The other Christians scrambled to put their hands over Kisuke's mouth and silence his cries. But in his lunatic state Kisuke had more than sufficient strength to brush off three or four men.

'Hey! I can't take it any more. I'll topple! Officer! I'll topple!'

The officer opened the thick cell door and lugged Kisuke out. The view they had of Kisuke from behind – being kicked and falling to the ground, falling and rising again and again as he was led away to the court – was hideous. He was taken before the officials to provide them with a fingerprint that would serve as proof that he had 'toppled'.

With a cold shudder Kanzaburō watched the retreating figure of his childhood friend as he was transformed into Judas, just as Kunitarō had prophesied. Once he had provided the officers with his thumbprint, Kisuke, no doubt ashamed, fled across the courtyard without even a glance towards the cell.

After Kisuke's apostasy, three other believers, unable to endure the *dodoi* torture, swore oaths to renounce their faith. It was painful to watch as trusted comrades one after another committed the act of betrayal. Perhaps even amidst their pain, the remaining thirty-four men had sealed a silent promise amongst themselves that they would never apostatize. They did not bend to any subsequent torture. The officers finally seemed to have given up, and for the time being ceased their physical abuse, and the men were moved to a tiny barracks in the Nagasaki hills, at a place called Kojima.

Three months passed. In October of that year, unbeknown to any of the prisoners, the Tokugawa shogunate collapsed.

Inevitably, foreign diplomats were distressed about the persecution of Kyushu Christians. They put considerable pressure on the new Meiji government to stop these incidents, but because the new rulers themselves had not yet decided on a policy towards religion, all they could do was give the same vague sort of reply that the shogunate had given in regard to Christianity. In reality, notice-boards were erected in Nagasaki neighbourhoods reading: 'Prohibition on Practice of Christianity Continues as Before. Practice of Heretical Beliefs Strictly Prohibited.' As a desperate measure the Meiji government broke with the defunct shogunate's practice of lumping Christianity together with 'heretical beliefs', and listed them separately.

But protests from various consular bodies rejected this wily tactic. Kido Takayoshi,[5] one of the Meiji oligarchs, took the matter seriously and changed the initial policy of punishing all the Christian faithful, deciding instead to exile only the prominent members of the flock to various provinces, then observing the attitudes of the remaining captives before deciding upon follow-up measures.

With these orders, twenty-eight of the thirty-eight prisoners from Nakano village were banished to Tsuwano in Iwami province. This took place in July, precisely one year after they were originally apprehended.

On the morning of 20 July, beneath a whitely shrouding morning mist, a small freighter awaited the criminals at the port of Nagasaki. Out in the offing a 1500-ton steamship stood ready. They were put on this vessel and transported as far as Onomichi. From there they proceeded to Hiroshima, then set out along the San'in highway over the mountains to Tsuwano.

5. Kido (1833–77) was instrumental in putting together a coalition of domains that toppled the Tokugawa shogunate and ushered in the Meiji restoration of 1867.

Just outside the castle town of Tsuwano is a hill known as Maiden Hill. The Kōrinji Temple erected on this hill became the prison where they were to live out the rest of their lives.

At first their lives at Kōrinji were relaxed. The officials, in their customary fashion, believed that because they were dealing with dirt-farmers it would be a simple matter to change the hearts of these men in short order merely by lecturing them thoroughly on religion. Their daily ration included five cups of rice, 73 mon worth of vegetables, and one square of paper, which for men who were no better than lowly peasants made for a tolerably comfortable life. Day after day, Buddhist clerics from the temple and Shintō priests came to sermonize to them. The Christians listened in silence to these lectures. When pressure was placed on them to apostatize, however, not one of them would nod his head in the affirmative. Finally the authorities had to subject them once again to torture.

The comparatively abundant ration of food they had been receiving was reduced to a single pinch of salt and a watery porridge. Their bedding was taken away and replaced with thin straw mats. Their clothing was restricted to the unlined summer kimonos they had been wearing when they were arrested.

Winter in the San'in turned bitter cold in October. The tortures were carried out next to the 65-square-metre pond in the garden of the Kōrinji. Stripped of their clothing, the Christians were stood one at a time beside the pond. Seventy-litre barrels filled with water were set beside them, and an officer with a long-handled dipper stood in wait.

'Then you will not apostatize?'

'I will not.' At that answer, each Christian was shoved into the pond, which was topped with a thin layer of ice. The water splashed as they struck it. When they floated to the surface, the officer jabbed at them with his dipper. Later on, Kanzaburō described the sufferings of that day as follows:

'My body turned cold and froze, and I began to shake and my teeth chattered, and I couldn't see any more. The world started spinning. Just when I felt I had breathed my last, the officer said: "Come out now." They had put a hook on the end of a metre-long bamboo shaft, and they coiled my hair round the end of the hook and pulled me in with all their might. Once they'd hauled me out of the water, they raked away the snow, and they built a log fire using two bundles of brushwood as kindling. They dried and warmed me there by the fire, then gave me some smelling-salts until I came to. I can't begin to describe the pain I felt that day.'

Once the water torture was completed, the prisoners were taken to the 1-metre cell. This was a one square-metre box, with bars of 6-centimetre-square poles placed at 3-centimetre intervals; the only opening was a hole at about eye-level for the providing of food. It was, of course, so cramped that the prisoners had to bend over before they could even crawl into the cell.

As a result of the tortures and the savage cold of the Tsuwano winter, the Christians began dying one after another. The first to die was a twenty-seven-year-old man named Wasaburō. He survived for twenty days in the 1-metre cell, but his strength finally failed and he died.

The next to die from the tortures was a thirty-two-year-old man named Yasutarō. To all appearances Yasutarō was a feeble fellow, but he went out of his way to offer the meagre food given him to others, and he willingly took on unpleasant chores such as cleaning their toilet. He was forced to sit out in the snow for three days and three nights, after which he was placed in the 1-metre cell, where he died with his body bent over.

Kanzaburō was able to speak with Yasutarō three days before his death. In one of his letters, Kanzaburō writes: 'I told him I thought he must be feeling very alone there in the tiny cell. But he answered: "No, I'm not at all lonely. Ever since I was nine years old, a person who looks just like Santa Maria, dressed in a blue kimono and veil, has told me stories, so I haven't been the least bit lonely. But please don't tell this to anyone while I'm still alive." And just three days after he said that to me, he died a truly noble death.'

With their comrades dying one after another, some of the surviving Christians began to lose heart. Finally, one particularly bitter winter night, sixteen men declared that they would forsake their faith. They were immediately released from the cell and given warm food and *sake*, and several days later they descended from the mountain.

Ten men remained. Included in their number were Kanzaburō and Zennosuke. There in the 1-metre cell they had to fight against their memories of the mountains, the houses and their families at home. More than anything else, these memories weakened their resolve.

'I wonder what's happened to Kisuke?' Sometimes Kanzaburō would think of the face and massive form of the friend he had not seen since they were together in the prison at Sakurachō. It was almost as if Kanzaburō could still see engraved on the back of his eyelids the retreating figure of Kisuke as the officers shoved him towards the court to offer his thumbprint. 'He's so cowardly. . . . If he weren't so spineless, Kisuke would have been able to hold on to his faith. . . .'

Around this time the officials came up with a new means to increase the torment of the ten Christians who had endured the water torture and the 1-metre cell. Their new strategy was to bring relatives of the believers to Tsuwano and to abuse them before the eyes of the men. The officials conjectured that it would be meaningless to torture the hearty brothers of their captives; it would be far more effective, they reasoned, to afflict their aged mothers and younger brothers and sisters.

In February twenty-six women and children were packed on to a ship and transported to Tsuwano. A new cell was assembled in the garden of the Kōrinji temple, and the newly arrived captives were placed in it.

Kanzaburō's younger sister, Matsu, and his younger brother, Yūjirō, were among the new prisoners. Matsu was fifteen and Yūjirō was twelve.

The children were tortured without mercy. A boy of ten called Suekichi refused to apostatize even though oil was poured on both his hands and they were set alight. A five-year-old child was fed nothing for two days, then taunted with sweets by the officers, but he merely shook his head firmly. His answer to the officers was: 'My mother told me that if I didn't give up Christianity I could go to Paradise, and that when I got to Paradise, they'd have things even more delicious than those sweets.'

Yūjirō was stripped naked and exposed to the frigid wind, where he was lashed to a cross made of logs and left to hang. At night an officer would throw water on him. He was beaten with whips. The whip handles were jabbed into his ears and nose. Being a child of twelve, he wailed in a loud voice that was clearly audible to Kanzaburō in his 1-metre cell. As elder brother he could offer no help other than his own prayers.

After a week Yūjirō's body began to turn pale and puffy. His heart had weakened. The alarmed officers ceased their tortures and turned him over to his sister Matsu. Gasping for breath with his head cradled in Matsu's lap, Yūjirō wept: 'Matsu, please forgive me. I tried not to cry like that. I thought about the Lord Jesus' torture and tried not to shout out. But it hurt so much, I ended up screaming. My faith is so weak, please forgive me, Matsu.'

Near dawn, clutching Matsu's hand, the young boy died. That morning the officers brought in a coffin, quickly placed the corpse inside it, and took it away without a word.

After his younger brother's murder, even Kanzaburō felt his heart was being ripped open. He didn't want to contemplate apostatizing, but it was unbearable to think that the same kind of torture might be applied to his sister Matsu.

'Why won't the Lord Jesus help us? Why does the Lord Jesus watch in silence while these children endure such horrible torture?' Doubts began to seep into his mind because the Lord gave them no answer in their extremity. He grew frightened of God's icy silence. It was at this time that Kanzaburō's faith began to waver.

'Why do we put up with this? What kind of religion makes you sacrifice your brothers and sisters?' Kanzaburō beat his head against the wooden poles of his 1-metre cell in order to drive away these haunting thoughts. The skin on his head split open and he began to bleed, but still he continued to strike his head on the pillar. Battering his head like this was the only means he had to overcome these frightening ideas. 'Zennosuke! Zennosuke!' he yelled to his friend. 'Pray for me!'

But no answer came, and he could not tell whether Zennosuke was alive or dead.

Four days after Yūjirō died, Kanzaburō decided that his heart could bear no more of this misery. Vacantly he stared through the hole in the cell door at the garden of the Kōrinji temple. An officer was talking with a man who appeared to be a beggar. The pauper's body was wrapped in a straw mat, and he leaned on a tall cane as he bowed his head over and over to the officer.

Kanzaburō felt as though he had seen that posture and that manner of bowing before. But he couldn't remember where.

Suddenly the officer raised his hand and beat the beggar roughly. The frightened beggar looked as though he were going to run away, but he staggered back two or three steps and halted.

Can that be Kisuke? Kanzaburō was astounded. Why in the world would Kisuke . . .?

But it was in fact Kisuke who came walking towards the cell after the officer sent him tottering. It was the same Kisuke who had staggered away from the prison at Sakura-chō in Nagasaki two years before.

Why has that coward Kisuke come here?

When the beggar passed in front of his cell, he appeared to have journeyed far before coming here to Tsuwano, and his face was pitch-black with whiskers and mud, but Kanzaburō could distinguish traces of the unforgettable bulk of his child-hood friend.

With a dull clatter the officer jerked the door of the cell open and shoved the beggar inside. After the officer left, there was silence for a long while. Eventually Kanzaburō shouted: 'Is that you, Kisuke? Is the man who just came into this cell by chance Kisuke of Nakano village?'

'Yes. . . .' A thin voice like the buzz of a mosquito responded. 'Yes. . . . Who are you?'

'It's me.' Rubbing his face against the opening in the cell,

Kanzaburō called out his name. 'Why did you come here? What in hell are you doing here?' His voice was flooded with all the spite and anger he had felt these several years towards his childhood friend. 'You gave them your fingerprint at the jail in Sakura-chō, so why have you come here?' No answer came for a time. Then at last a dull-witted answer reached his ears. It was Kisuke's voice, pleading as if through tears.

'Please forgive me. Please forgive me.'

Then falteringly Kisuke began to explain to Kanzaburō. Everyone in the cell listened quietly to his words. From time to time as Kisuke spoke they heard the footsteps of the guards, and in fear Kisuke would stop speaking. At nightfall the cold became even more bitter, and a powdery snow began to fall.

After Kisuke, unable to bear the cries of his comrades as they suffered the *dodoi* torture at Sakura-chō, had offered his fingerprint to the officials, he could no longer return to Nakano village. He wanted to see his parents and sisters, but the shame of having betrayed his faith and the pain of having abandoned his friends forced him to take refuge in Nagasaki. There he had worked as a stevedore in the great harbour.

'I reckoned I'd been forsaken by the Lord and by Santa Maria, so I abandoned myself to *sake* and evil activities to try to forget about all of you.'

As a tearful Kisuke made his confession, the men in the cell sighed and nodded their heads.

Though he drank *sake* and paid for women, Kisuke was unable to forget the agony in his heart. But at this point he could no longer go to the authorities and retract his declaration of apostasy, thereby declaring himself a Christian once again. His cowardice prevented him from making such a declaration and having to listen again to the screams of those undergoing the *dodoi* torture. Those dark, bestial cries still echoed hauntingly at the core of his ears. To block out those voices Kisuke fled from Nagasaki to the fishing village of Shirogoe. There he took on work with a fisherman's family. He felt the physical exhaustion that came from rowing a boat and hauling in ropes would be a better means than *sake* and women to quell the pain in his heart.

But one day when Kisuke and his employer brought a catch of fish to Nagasaki for the first time in several months, he had to witness an unexpected scene. Officers at the dock were shoving prisoners on to two freighters. Pelted with jeers from the assembled crowd and poked with poles by the officers, the prisoners were driven like animals on to the boats. Kisuke stood on his toes and peered over the shoulders of the crowd, and there he saw that the prisoners were women and children he knew from Nakano village. The familiar faces of Matsu and Yūjirō were among the captives. Their eyes were lowered in grief, and with drooping heads they sat down without a word in the water-soaked ship.

'Those are Christian prisoners.' Kisuke's employer poked his shoulder. 'They're fools, aren't they?'

Kisuke averted his eyes and nodded to his employer, who was staring into his face.

That night he went out on to the sea-shore and sat alone staring at the dark ocean.

What can a coward like me do? A coward like me?

Listening to the sound of the dark waves that pushed in and broke, broke and then retreated, Kisuke felt a bitterness towards God surging up from the depths of his heart. There are two types of people – those born with strong hearts and courage, and those who are craven and clumsy. From their childhood Kanzaburō and Zennosuke had been strong of will. So even when they were subjected to persecution, they had been able to maintain their faith. But me – I'm spineless by nature, and my knees buckle and I turn pale if someone just lifts a hand against me. Because I was born like that, even though I want to believe in the Lord Jesus' teachings, in no way can I put up with torture.

If only I hadn't been born in these times. . . .

If Kisuke had lived in the distant past when freedom of religion was accessible, even if he had not been one of the valiant souls, he wouldn't have ended up in this predicament of betraying the Lord Jesus and Santa Maria.

Why was I born to such a fate?

That thought made Kisuke resent God's lack of compassion.

It happened just as Kisuke stood and was about to leave the beach. He heard a voice calling to him from behind. He turned round, but no one was there. It was neither the voice of a man nor a woman. But he had heard the voice echoing clearly amidst the sound of the black ocean waves.

'All you have to do is go and be with the others. If you're tortured again and you become afraid, it's all right to run away. It's all right to betray me. But go follow the others.'

Kisuke stopped in his tracks and looked out at the sea in a daze. He pressed his fists against his face and wept aloud.

When Kisuke had finished his story, the Christians in the cell were silent, emitting not even a cough. As they sat in confinement they knew from the sharp stab at their skin that the snow was gradually piling up outside. Kanzaburō felt that the tortures he had endured these two years, and the fact that his brother had died without abandoning the faith, had not been in vain.

The next morning the officers unlocked the door to the 1-metre cell to interrogate Kisuke. If Kisuke would not agree to apostatize, he would be thrown into the icy lake in the garden of the temple. As he listened to the rasp of the lock and to Kisuke's faltering footsteps, Kanzaburō whispered: 'Kisuke. If it hurts you, it's all right to apostatize. It's all right. The Lord Jesus is pleased just because you came here. He is pleased.'

Shadows

I don't know whether I'll actually send this letter. I've already written you something like three letters. But I've either broken them off half-way, or, if I've been able to finish them, I've stuck them in my desk drawer and never mailed them to you.

Each time I've tried writing to you, I found myself wondering if in fact the letter is not meant for you but addressed to myself, to calm my anxieties and bring some degree of understanding to my mind. Ultimately the reason I never sent any of the letters I wrote is probably because I felt the act of writing was pointless, and brought no satisfaction to the depths of my heart. But circumstances are somewhat different now. I feel now that a gradual understanding, though imperfect, is budding in my mind with regard to what you did.

Where can I begin? Should I start with my recollections of meeting you in my childhood, when you first arrived in Japan? Or should I begin with the day my mother died, when you opened the front door for me after I raced home, only to shake your head and say 'She's gone.'

As a matter of fact, I ran into you yesterday. You of course had no idea that I was there, or that you were being watched. As you sat at the table waiting for your food to be brought, you pulled a book from your old black bag (I remember that bag) and began reading. That reminded me of the way, when you were a priest, you would take out your breviary before meals and open it up. We were at a small restaurant in Shibuya, and the pedestrians walking in the drizzling rain outside the clouded window looked like fish in an aquarium. I sat with the sports page of the newspaper spread out, shovelling curry rice into my mouth with one hand. The news that one of my favourite players in the Taiyō team was going to be traded was announced in large lettering. At the bottom of the page, a novel by a friend of mine was being serialized.

When I glanced up, a foreigner dressed in black with his back towards me was about to sit down in a corner of the restaurant. I was startled. I hadn't seen you in six years. Our seats were separated by some 20 metres, while between us four or five businessmen at the same table were eating hamburger steaks.

'. . . The gears in that car are hard to operate, aren't they?'

'I don't think so. . . .'

Those fragments of conversation reached my ears. One of them had a dark-red blemish the size of a 10-yen coin on his balding forehead.

You gave an affable smile to the young waitress who brought you a glass of water, then pointed to something on the menu. The waitress nodded and left, and then you pulled an English book out of your old black bag and began reading. Actually, I don't know if it was in English, but it was written in horizontal lines. He's got really old, I thought. He's a decrepit old man. To say this is to run the risk of offending a man who had served as a missionary, but in your youthful days you were truly a handsome rogue. I can still remember that when I first met you in the Kōbe hospital and saw your deep-etched face and your wine-coloured eyes; even as a child I thought what a splendid man you were. Now that face has been eroded by age, your chestnut hair has thinned (my own, I admit, is rather sparse), and your cheeks just below your eyes are red and puffy, as though celluloid bags had been implanted there. In that face I tried to sniff out the loneliness that has been yours since the incident. I tried to ascertain your struggles since you took on the burdens of a wife and children and had to find a job in a foreign land, and the pain you've had to endure after losing your friends and anyone who might help you.

I wanted to stand up and walk over to you and say: 'Hello,

it's been a long time!' But I remained in my chair, unable to speak to you, and like a detective in an investigation bureau, I hid my face behind the newspaper and scrutinized you. Certainly curiosity was at work. And my interest in human behaviour as a novelist played a part, too. But there was more to it. Some powerful force in my mind held me back and prevented me from coming over to you. I'm planning to write about the power that restrained me in this letter. In any case, I sat there spying on you. Finally the waitress brought you a plate full of food. You nodded and smiled as you had before, then tucked a handkerchief into your shirt in place of a napkin. I was still watching you intently. You straightened your chair and sat up squarely in it. And then you brought your fingers up to your chest, and quickly, so that no one would notice, you crossed yourself. An inexpressible emotion surged through me at that moment. 'So, you're still like that, after all?'

The force that stopped me from going to your table – it's hard to explain what it was. Because, to put it in different terms, it's one of the major rivers that have given shape to my life. I've written a number of different novels over the years by thrusting my hands into those rivers. I've plucked up objects that have been deposited at the bottom of my river, washed the dirt from them, and arranged them all together. There are many important objects there that I still haven't dredged up. I haven't yet written anything about my father, whom you never met, or my mother, whom you looked after in so many ways throughout her life. Nor have I yet turned my hand to a depiction of you. No, that's not true. Since I first became a novelist, I've changed various details about your life and written about you on three different occasions. Over the many years since that incident, you have been an important narrative figure for me. Even though you're such a crucial character, virtually every story I've written about you has been a failure. I know why. It's because I still didn't have a firm grasp of who you are. Yet, though the failures continued to mount, you never ceased to hover around the world of my mind. How comfortable things would have been for me if I'd been able to chase you out. But how could I possibly drive away my mother and you?

Whenever I look back along the river of my life, somehow I always think of that little church in the Hanshin district where I was compelled to receive baptism. That tiny little Catholic church, it remains unchanged even today. The pseudo-Gothic steeple, the gold cross, the oleanders in the garden. As you know, my mother had separated from my father because of her tempestuous personality, and she took me back to Japan from Dalian in Manchuria, and we moved in with her elder sister in Hanshin. This sister was a devout Christian, and at her encouragement Mother began to seek healing of her desolate heart through faith. Of necessity I began attending the church, escorted there by my mother and aunt. A French priest was in charge of the church. As the war grew more fierce, one day this priest from the Pyrenees was hauled off by two military policemen who had stormed into the church. He was suspected of being a spy.

But all that happened much later. The war had already started in China, but times had not yet become that difficult for the Catholic Church in Japan. At Christmas they could still ring out the hallelujah bells in the depths of the night, and on Easter Sunday flowers adorned the gates and doors of the church, and we beamed with pride while mischievous boys from the neighbourhood looked on enviously at the young girls decked out in white veils like those the foreign girls wear. One Easter day, the French priest lined up ten children and asked each of them: 'Do you believe in Christ?' And each of them parroted back: 'I believe.' I was one of those children. Imitating the voices of the other children, I loudly called out: 'Yes, I believe.'

During the summer holiday, one of the seminarists at the church often performed stories for us with illustrations drawn on paper. He also took us hiking up Mt Rokkō. After he returned to his home, we boys would frequently play catch in the garden of the church. Once when someone missed the ball it struck a window, and the French priest thrust his enraged face through the window and screamed at us. Not every day was a happy one for me, because my mother, separated from Father, would often sit with a dark expression on her face as she discussed something or other with my aunt. But unlike the time we were living in Dalian, I was spared the torment of suffering alone while my parents fought, and I think it was a relatively stable period for me.

Once in a while an old foreigner would come to the church. He would pick a time when none of the members were there, but while we were playing baseball we saw him sneaking into the priest's quarters. 'Who is that?' I asked my aunt and mother, but for some reason they averted their eyes and said nothing. But one of my friends told me about the man, who dragged one of his legs as he walked. 'He was kicked out.' Although he had been a priest, he had married a Japanese woman; because he had been expelled from the Church, none of the members would ever say a word about him, and they clamped their mouths shut, as though the very mention of his name would sully their faith. The only person who would meet him was the priest from the Pyrenees. As for me, I stole glances at the old man with feelings that combined fear with curiosity and a certain enjoyment. Having spent my childhood in Dalian, in that emigrant colony I had seen several old White Russians who had been driven from their homeland, and the face of one of those old men who had come to the Japanese settlement selling Russian bread reminded me of this man. Both of them wore overcoats that gave the impression less that they were worn than that they were demolished; around their necks both wore large, hand-knitted scarves, and they both dragged their rheumatic legs and stopped from time to time to wipe their noses with large, filthy handkerchiefs. Thinking back on them now, I realize that the lonely shadows clouding their faces were similarly imbued with the pain of those who have been exiled from the thing that has sustained the very core of their lives.

It was an evening during the summer holiday. I was walking along a road. I suppose I must have been on my way to play baseball. In front of the gate to the church, brightly illuminated by the twilight sun, I nearly ran smack into the old man. It never occurred to me that he might come out from the church.

In surprise, I stood frozen, my body stiffened like a rock. The old man said something to me, but I had no idea what it was. I was filled with feelings of revulsion and fear. I shook my head and made a quick attempt to race up the stone steps leading to the chapel. But a large hand gripped my shoulder. 'Not to worry', or 'Nothing to be scared' – the old man said something of the kind to me in broken Japanese. His breath was foul. In desperation I fled. All I could remember was the sad look in his wine-coloured eyes as he gazed at me then. When I got home I told my mother what had happened, but she said nothing. After two or three days, I too had forgotten all about it.

Strangely enough, only a month after this incident occurred you came into my life. I can't help but feel now that this coincidence has had great meaning in the river of my life. A year ago, as I was composing a long novel, I frequently pondered that coincidence. In the novel, I had my protagonist compare the weary, haggard, worn and sunken face of Christ in the *fumie* with the face of Christ that appears in Western devotional painting – the face filled with tranquillity, purity and fervour. As I composed those scenes, the images that surfaced in my mind were of your face from then, and the face of that outcast old man.

The autumn of that same year, I developed appendicitis and had to enter the Charity Hospital at Nada. After my stitches were removed, my aunt and mother were feeding me rice gruel when you suddenly came into my hospital room. The two women stood up in surprise. They were not taken aback because a priest had come in. The only priests we had ever seen, whether the priest at our church or any other father, had all been scrawny men wearing thick spectacles. The Japanese fathers in particular always looked so peculiar we couldn't decide whether they were Japanese or Nisei. When you opened that door and came in the room, you were completely different from the others. With your solid body clothed in a well-kept black suit with a pure white Roman collar and a gentlemanly smile on your well-nourished face, you were enough to throw the three of us Japanese into a state of confusion. After giving a polite greeting to my aunt and mother, you looked down at me. I lay there stiff as a rock, still clutching my chopsticks and rice-bowl in my hands. Your Japanese was very fluent. Sweat beaded my forehead as I tried earnestly to answer your questions. 'Yes, I'm well now.' 'No, I'm not lonely.' After you left, I cried out 'What a handsome man!' and my mother heaved a deep sigh. 'What a pity that a man like that became a priest and can't get married.' My aunt chided my mother for her impious remark.

But it seems that my mother did take a great deal of interest in you. When she came to visit my room, without fail she would ask whether you had been in to see me.

'You're such a bother. For God's sake leave me alone!' Feeling somehow ill at ease, I was intentionally rude to her. But out of feminine curiosity my mother learned that you had been a soldier who graduated from the military academy in Spain, that you'd had a change of heart and abandoned the military in order to follow the path of a priest, that you had gone to seminary, and that after coming to Japan you had spent a year at a monastery in Kakogawa.

'He's not like your ordinary priests. He was born into a scholar's family. I can imagine how truly happy it must make his mother to have a splendid son like him.'

Mother said this to encourage me, but even as a child I could sense that these were not words directed exclusively at her son.

Even after I was released, Mother frequently brought me to the hospital. She was not satisfied with what the run-of-the-mill priests had to say. Though she had in fact been baptized, with her stern character she must have felt that something she starved for had been satisfied when you suddenly appeared in front of her. My father, who was cautious and preferred to tread the asphalt highway of a circumspect life, had been unable to bear the way my mother lived. Christianity, to which my mother had drawn near at her sister's encouragement to assuage her temporary solitude, began at this point in time to become something true to her. Besides teaching music at several schools in the Hanshin region, she began devouring the books that you lent her one after another. And from that time her life changed completely. She demanded of herself a strict life of prayer, like a nun's existence, and required the same of me. Each morning she took me to mass, and in every free moment she recited her rosary. She even seemed to have started thinking about bringing me up to become a priest like you.

I have no intention of writing about the spiritual association between you and my mother. But two years later, you began visiting our home every Saturday as my aunt's and my mother's guidance priest. Friends of my aunt and members of the church also assembled there. I can admit this to you now: the days when you came over were very painful for me. Mother became even more stern than usual, and made me wash my hands and get my hair cut, and she gave me strict orders, saying: 'Now you behave yourself properly when Father comes over.' Even worse, how was I supposed to understand anything you said there amongst the adults? Whether because I was nervous, or because I was prone to tiredness (you are well aware of how physically weak I've been from childhood), it took all my energy to fight off drowsiness as I sat beside my mother. Who cares anything about the Old Testament or the New Testament or Christ or Moses? I did everything I could think of – pinching my knees, thinking about something else – to fight the boredom and my increasingly heavy eyelids. My mother glared at me with fearsome eyes. I was able to stay awake for the full hour from dread of that gaze.

On summer mornings without fail, and even on wintry mornings, my mother never allowed me to miss going to church. 5:30 a.m. While darkness still clung to most of the sky and every house was fast asleep, I would walk behind her as she silently prayed, blowing on my hands to warm them as we made our way along the frost-frozen road to the church. Beside the feeble candle at the altar the French priest hunched over, his hands clasped, and recited the mass, his shadow etched against the wall. The only people kneeling within the frigid chapel were two old women, my mother and I. When I nodded off as I pretended to pray, Mother would glare at me with a frightening face.

'Do you think you can become like the Father if you behave like that?'

'The Father', of course, was you. To her you had become the idealized image of my future, the portrait of the man I was impelled to become. Of necessity I developed a revulsion towards you, and I grew sick of your immaculate clothes, your well-cared-for face and fingers. I could no longer stand your proud smile, your learning, or your faith. Do you remember, that it was around this time my grades at school began to drop? I was in my second year of middle school, but I consciously set out to become a lazy, slovenly boy. Because a lazy, slovenly person was indisputably the opposite of what you were. In rebellion against my mother for trying to fashion me into a man like you who lived with profound conviction and confidence in your faith and your way of life, I purposely went out of my way to neglect my studies and become as poor a student as I could. When Mother was around I made as though I was busy at my study desk, but I did absolutely nothing.

I had a dog then. He was a mongrel I got from the eel-shop owner in our neighbourhood. Without any siblings, and having no friends with whom I could share my sorrow over the complicated rift between my parents, I showered affection on this dim-witted dog. Dogs and little birds still appear frequently in my fiction, but they are no mere decorations. In those days the only one I felt really understood my inexpressible loneliness was this mongrel. Even today, the moist, grieving eyes of dogs somehow remind me of the eyes of Christ. This Christ I speak of is, of course, not the Christ filled with assurance of his own way of life, as you once were. It is the weary Christ of the *fumie*, trampled upon by men and looking up at them from beneath their feet.

As was her habit, my mother began to berate me for the decline in my grades. Evidently she sought counsel from you about this. With a faintly stern expression, you cautioned me to study diligently so that my mother would not worry. Inside my heart I muttered: 'What the hell do you know? You're just a stupid foreigner.' I set myself to become even more idle precisely because you were the one who admonished me to do better. One day you apparently told my aunt and my mother that in Western households children are punished a bit more frequently, that appropriate discipline is meted out to children who fail to make appropriate effort. And to punish me when my grades remained at the same low level during the third term, you ordered my mother to get rid of my dog.

I can still vividly remember my anguish then. Naturally I lent no ear to her orders. But one day when I returned home from school, my beloved pet was gone. She had got some boy in the neighbourhood to drag him away. I'm sure you don't even remember this. To you the dog was nothing more than a deterrent that took my attention away from my studies, and I'm sure you felt that getting rid of the dog was for my own good. Of course I do not resent you for that. But one reason I bring up such trifling matters here is because they seem so typical of you. More than anything else, you hated weakness, laziness and sloppiness in yourself and in others. I imagine it's because that's how your family was. Or perhaps your training as a soldier made you like that. 'A man must be strong. He must constantly strive. He must steel himself in his life and in his beliefs.' You never said as much in words, but you practised these principles in your life. Everyone knows how energetically you threw yourself into your proselytizing work, how unflaggingly you studied theology. There is no room for criticism. Everyone (my mother included) looked up to you as a splendid human being. In my own childish way, I was the only one who began to suffer because of your unassailable goodness.

Unfortunately for me, you took on a new responsibility around that time. A dormitory for Christian students was erected on a hill at Mikage, and you were relieved of your duties as full-time priest at the Charity Hospital so that you could become the resident priest at this dormitory. 'I'm really not cut out for this kind of job,' you explained with a perplexed look to the people who had gathered for their regular instruction in the Bible. 'But I have to do it, since the orders came from above.' In spite of your denials, you seemed to be interested in the job. On our way home my mother suddenly asked me if I would like to move into your dormitory. She felt that, if I just lived beside you, my plummeting grades would return to their previous level, and that I would also grow in faith. I told her again and again that I didn't want to, but you remember how strong-willed she was. When I came home later that year with yet another disgraceful report card, I was placed in the dormitory where you had already been serving as dorm master for six months.

It was an austere lodging. I suppose you must have taken a Western seminary dormitory or a military academy barracks as your model. I'm not trying to make any excuses, but I really did make some effort. Yet everything turned out just the opposite of what you had hoped for me. I couldn't accept that the things you considered 'for my own good' were really so. Even things I did with no ill intentions whatsoever you viewed as signs of my weakness. You tried to steel me, to hammer me into shape 'for Mother's benefit'. You never realized that the hammer might eventually crush me.

There would be no end to it were I to begin writing down each of those episodes. Do you remember when this happened? The dorm students (most of whom were college students; only I and another fellow, N, were still in middle school) would get up every morning at six and go to mass, after which one of our daily duties was to jog along the mountain path behind the dorm to breakfast. I couldn't bear that. I'm sure it was nothing to you, after your military training, or to the college students at the dorm. But having weak bronchial tubes since childhood, I would be panting for breath in no time, and my eyes would begin to swim. After the run, greasy sweat painted my forehead, and I had lost all appetite for food, and sometimes I even felt light-headed. I came up with clever ways of avoiding running. But you finally found me out. You told me there was no reason why I shouldn't be doing exactly the same thing that the other middle-school boy, N, was doing. But with your robust physique, you could not understand how hard it was for someone physically weak like me to participate in that kind of training. 'Everyone is running to build up their bodies. You're just not making the effort.' That was your side of the story. To you I appeared to be a selfish boy with a dislike for group training.

Then we'd head off to our various schools, and when we returned, after dinner you lectured to us. I often dropped off to sleep. I dozed during evening prayers in the chapel afterwards. With my frail constitution I got pretty worn out from the classes and military drill at school during the day, so I could get nothing out of an even more trying lecture on theology.

On one such evening, while everyone else was listening to your sermon, I was as always nodding off to sleep. Even though I was in the far back corner, I suppose I must have been snoring lightly too. You realized I had fallen asleep and you suddenly broke off your sermon. N, who was sitting beside me, poked me in the side, and I opened my eyes in surprise. To my embarrassment, I had drooled down my chin and soaked my jacket. At first everyone laughed, but when they noticed your stern look they suddenly turned silent. You unexpectedly raised one hand and shouted at me in Japanese: 'Get out!'

That was the first time I saw you turn red and yell in anger. Normally you greeted my mother and aunt and the other believers with a gentlemanly smile, and this was the first time I saw your face twisted in rage. You were not angry with me for falling asleep. Later you explained to my mother that you had blown up at me because I was using my physical frailty as a general excuse for not conducting my life the way your dormitory students were expected to. That's certainly true. I admit that I didn't follow the daily routine at the dormitory whenever I could get out of it. I acknowledge that, as you claimed, I didn't try my hardest. But it's also a fact that I was physically unable to endure the kind of life you conceived as ideal. I'm not making excuses for the way I behaved then. All I'm trying to say is that your good intentions and determination, though they had positive results with those who were strong, for the weak were at times cruel, and instead of producing positive results simply inflicted unnecessary scars.

Finally, after less than ten months, I left your dormitory and returned to my mother's house. Still, being a mother, she struggled to discern some strong qualities or virtues in her useless son, but by then you seemed to feel nothing but disappointment and scorn for me. Your behaviour towards me certainly didn't change from what it had been, but you began to speak to me less often. In this manner, my mother's dream – her dream of making me into a priest like you – was shattered.

As I read over what I have written here, I fear that you may misunderstand me. I have in no way forgotten the kindness you extended to Mother and me. Far from it; I believe it was because of you that she was rescued from despair after her divorce, and because of you that she was able to immerse herself in the Christianity that sustained her spirit until her death. I always feel grateful to you for helping her in so many ways until she died.

What I'm trying to say is completely different. If there are the strong and the weak among human beings, in those days you were truly one of the strong. And I was a spineless weakling. You had confidence in your way of life, in your faith, in your body, and you performed your missionary work in Japan with firm conviction. In contrast, not once in my life have I been able to feel confidence and conviction about every facet of my life. As I say this, I imagine that in your current state you will understand everything. But in the past you would have resolutely shaken your head in disagreement. You would have shaken your head, and in a loud voice you would have cried that man exists so that he can strive to reach ever greater heights throughout his life. But weren't you forced to learn, some fifteen years later, that unexpected perils and danger spots like thin ice lurk within such strength, and that amidst such perils come the beginnings of true religion?

My mother died after I finished middle school and was entering into my second year in limbo, still unable to get into any higher school. I took one entrance exam and failed, then another and failed, until finally even Mother got tired of reprimanding me and would just heave deep sighs. When I remember that look on her face, even now it pains me to the heart. She began to tire easily and started to complain of occasional dizziness. When you took her to the hospital one day, the doctor found that her blood pressure was very high, but she refused to stop pushing herself, and she never missed morning mass or relaxed her demanding way of life.

At the moment my mother died, I was seeing a film with a friend. I had deceived her by telling her that I was attending a college preparatory school, when in fact I was spending most of the day with friends at coffee shops and cinemas in Sannomiya. It was the end of December, and when I came out of the cinema it was pitch-black outside. I phoned home, planning to lie to Mother and tell her that we had been taking a practice test. To my surprise, the person who answered the phone was you. Mother had collapsed in the street, and you came rushing over as soon as you were notified. I learned for the first time that you had organized several groups of people to go out looking for me. When you asked 'Where are you?' I quickly hung up the phone. How sluggish the Hankyū train taking me back home seemed! I had never raced home from the station so quickly. When I rang the bell, you were the one who opened the door for me. 'She's gone' was all you muttered. Mother had been placed upon her bed; faint traces of agony were still lingering between her brows. My aunt and some people from the church had assembled there, and sensing their accusing eyes on me, I stared at Mother's waxy face. My mind was curiously clear, and in that moment I felt no pain or sorrow. I was merely at a loss. You said nothing to me. Only the others were able to weep.

When everyone went home after her funeral, my aunt and you and I were left alone in the empty house. A decision had to be made about what to do with me. You were in more of a daze than I was. You seemed in a stupor, as though you had lost something that had previously been yours. So when my aunt asked me what I wanted to do, I told her that I didn't want to be a burden to anyone else. Then she suggested my father. Finally you lifted your bewildered face and expressed your view that everything should be handled according to my wishes. It was decided that you would explain the situation to my father.

I left the disposal of Mother's house to you and my aunt and returned to my father's home in Tokyo. From that day I began a life with a father and his new wife, towards neither of whom I could feel any affection as my parents.

After attempting to live with Father, I began to understand why Mother had left him. He was constantly saying things like 'Mediocrity is the best way. The greatest happiness lies in not making waves.' On days when he took a holiday from the company he managed, he would toy with his *bonsai* trees, tend the lawn in his yard, listen to a baseball game on the radio – that was his life. Every day he made some sort of effort to persuade me to choose the safe path of the businessman in my future. It was nothing like the rigorous daily life I had spent when there were only my mother and I. At her house, I was awakened each winter morning and walked down the frost-hardened path to the church. In the dark chapel where our only companions were the two elderly women, the French priest faced the cross, upon which Christ shed his blood. But in Father's house, not a word was ever said about life or religion, and the only topics of discussion were how noisy the neighbour's radio was, or how meagre the rations of rice had become. Mother had tried to inculcate in me the belief that holy things were the most exalted and wonderful things upon the face of this earth. But the atmosphere at Father's suggested that any mention of such things would cause them to turn the other way, even to ridicule me. Living in what were considerably better material circumstances, I felt every single day that I was betraying Mother. It was painful, but not a day went by that I didn't think about the mother who now seemed very dear to me. The only things that served as meagre compensation for the pangs of conscience I suffered were the letters I wrote to you. Because you had been the person Mother most respected up to the day of her death. By composing letters to you, I felt as though I were being saved, if even for a moment, from the self-reproach that came from knowing that I was in the process of betraying her wishes for me.

From time to time you would send a brief reply. Father

snarled every time he saw an envelope addressed in your hand. I'm sure it must have bothered him to have memories of Mother still in his son's head, to have her words still lingering there, to have me feel close to her friends. Looking away from me, he muttered in annoyance: 'You shouldn't associate with one of those useless "Amen" priests.' The following year, when I was somehow able to squeak my way into a private university, you notified me that you were taking up a position at a theology school in Tokyo.

It's the middle of the night. While my wife and child sleep, I sit up by myself in the house and resurrect each segment of my past so that I can write this letter. But as I read through what I have already written, I am amazed at the overwhelming number of incidents I haven't been able to write about. I realize even more emphatically now how difficult it is to talk about you, and to talk about my mother. In order to write down everything, I shall have to wait until the day comes when individuals will not be wounded by it – no, even more important, I shall have to write everything about myself. That is how inseparably tied my life is to you and Mother, how deeply the two of you have sunk your roots into me. Eventually, I suppose, I shall be able to describe in my own fiction the marks that you and Mother left upon me, and examine their essence.

But I must go back to where I left off if I am to continue this rough sketch. I went to see you as soon as you came to Tokyo. You hadn't changed at all. You didn't even have the pale complexion of other Fathers and seminarists. Your shoes were meticulously polished, the suit that encased your large body was carefully brushed and pressed, and you still spoke in the same confident manner. You were pleased that I had finally been accepted into college. 'Do you believe in Christ? Are you still going to mass?' When I said nothing, you looked displeased. 'I know you're not too busy. Or are you using the old excuse that you're too physically weak?' Tinges of disappointment and contempt surfaced on your face, just as they had when I left your dormitory.

That elicited the same feelings of defiance I had experienced in my childhood. But, partly because you were very busy with your new job at the seminary, our meetings gradually became less and less frequent. Not that you ever ceased to exist within my mind. Even as I continued to live with my father, my attachment to Mother grew all the deeper, and the resentment I had once felt towards her was transformed into fond remembrance, and I even idealized her fervent personality. At the very least, she instilled into the very depths of my soul that even a laggard like me had to live on a higher plane of existence. And you, at the very least, constituted a major portion of what Mother was. I think I must have enrolled in the literature department at my college because I had observed the way she lived. It must have had something to do with my realization that the kind of life you and Mother led was a world apart from the lives of most people, including my father. The less my life was like yours, the more distant it became, the more frequently I would think of you and feel ashamed.

Ultimately the war drove an even broader wedge between us. One day I got an unexpected letter from you informing me that you had been forced to leave Tokyo and live in Karuizawa. You and the rest of the foreign priests had been compelled by the Japanese authorities to evacuate to Karuizawa. Although it was called 'evacuation', clearly you lived a kind of concentration camp existence, being under constant watch of the Japanese MPs and police.

Around the same times, classes were cancelled at my school, and I was assigned to produce aircraft parts for Zero fighters while I cowered in fear of air raids at a plant in Kawasaki. It was no easy task even to buy a train ticket to Karuizawa. But one day, with a ticket finally in hand, I set out for that tiny village in Shinshū province. I still remember that when I got off the train the cold seemed sharp enough to slash my cheeks. This resort town, which must have been bustling in times of peace, was utterly desolate, darkly silent and gloomy. Two sharp-eyed men were warming themselves at a brazier in the MP office across from the station. A woeful plume of smoke rose from a grove of larch trees where some refugees were boiling a pot of rice porridge. I called at the office of the neighbourhood association, and guided by the neighbourhood chief I was able to find the large, wooden, Western-style building where you and your comrades were staying. We were reunited in the frozen garden. The chief stood a little apart from us, with his back turned, while you said: 'You aren't skipping mass, are you? You must believe in Christ.' Even here your clothing, though thoroughly reduced to tatters, was carefully brushed. But your hands were swollen with frost-bite. You went back into the building, and soon came out again with a package wrapped in newspaper.

'Take this back with you,' you said quickly, placing the bundle in my hands. The chief noticed this and approached suspiciously. 'What is that?' Angrily you replied: 'It's my ration of butter. Is there anything wrong with giving him something that belongs to me?'

The war ended. You returned to Tokyo from Karuizawa, and I avoided the draft just before being snatched up and was able to go back to my broken-down college from the factory where I had been obliged to work. A new age dawned for Christianity in Japan. The priests like yourself, who had been forced to evacuate during the war under suspicion from the police that they were spies, began now to perform their missionary work with impunity, and some Japanese began to attend church in search of the power to live, while others came out of desire for food and material possessions, while yet others came to have contact with foreigners. I often saw you in those days driving out of the seminary at the wheel of a jeep; you were very busy then. It was your responsibility to enlarge the seminary, which had been very small before. When I came to see you in your semicircular office, one of the rare Quonset huts around in those days, your secretary was busily handling the telephone calls that were coming in rapid succession. 'I'm sorry, but the Father isn't in at the moment,' she would often curtly reply. 'I'm afraid I have no idea when he'll be able to see you.'

None of this really matters. I write down such inane details because I hesitate to touch on what is really the central concern of my letter. I've now come to the stage where I must relate it, and I can sense the point of my brush dulling. The fear that I will wound you deeply has restrained me in what I have written thus far. Please forgive me.

But how should I phrase it? Exactly how did it happen? Even now I have no idea. I don't know how to interpret what gradually took place within your heart. Somerset Maugham has a novel called *Rain*, in which a clergyman bit by bit violates the restrictions on his behaviour and begins to love a woman. Maugham attempts to explain that whole process from without, using the image of long, monotonous rain. As a literary technique it is superb, but I cannot bring myself to employ such manipulation when I think about what you did. After it happened, everyone was saying: 'I can't believe it. . . . That's absolutely impossible!' I didn't believe it either. But it was true. And today, many years after the event, I still have no idea how to pursue the changes that occurred in your thinking.

It happened shortly after I finished college. I was still living at my father's, managing to get by one way or another by doing translations for fashion and technical magazines. Though I wanted to establish myself as a writer, I still had no confidence that I could become a novelist. And in the attempt to dodge the string of possible marriage candidates that my father paraded before me, I drew close to a young woman towards whom I felt very little emotion. I had only one condition that I required of this young woman, who later became my wife. 'I'm a useless Christian myself, but if you are going to marry me, I can't have you being indifferent to my religion.' I somehow held on to my faith because of my attachment to Mother. So even though I sometimes played truant from mass and kept my distance from church, I revered the faith that my mother believed and that you lived for, and never for a moment did I consider tossing it aside. So I came to see you to ask if you would teach this young woman the doctrines of Christianity.

A trace of surprise crossed your face. I don't know if you were surprised that a fellow like me had become engaged, or if you hadn't expected someone like me to step out of character and impel another person to study Christianity. You agreed, of course, but at the time I noticed something strange. You had grown just a little bit of a scruffy beard, and your shoes were not well polished. That slackness would have seemed like nothing at all in another priest, but I couldn't imagine it happening with you. During the long war, and even during your internment at Karuizawa, you had displayed the force of your will in your raiment. Your well-brushed shoes, cleansed of every trace of dirt. You had sternly ordered each of us in the dormitory to follow your example. From my own slovenliness, I at once loathed you and held you in awe. You escorted me and the young woman to the door. There, a woman was talking to your secretary. She wore a kimono and her complexion was pallid. From a Japanese perspective, she could not have been called a beautiful woman.

Alone I boarded a packed train and set out for the Hanshin region where I had lived with Mother. Memories of my mother were spreading their roots deeply in my mind, and I had decided to report my engagement, which I still kept secret from Father, only at Mother's grave. The neighbourhood where my house once stood had been reduced to ashes by the bombing raids, my aunt's family had decided to remain in Kagawa prefecture where they were evacuated, and the majority of friends I tried calling on had disappeared. All that remained unchanged from the past were the road I had silently walked along towards the church with my mother on dark winter mornings, and the church itself. In place of the French priest, now a Japanese Father in like manner intoned mass by himself in the deserted chapel, his shadow dancing on the walls in the light from the candles. I stood in front of the house where I lived with my mother (the house was now owned by someone from Taiwan or Korea), and I remembered your hollow face after Mother's funeral. I wondered why I had felt that a look of loss had appeared in your face, too. Then I had a glance at the pine grove where I had roamed in search of the dog you made me give up. The moist, sad expression in that dog's eyes suddenly flickered through my mind. A yellow whirlwind twisted through the burnt ruins, while an exhausted-looking man dug in the ground with a spade.

It was around this time that I first heard the preposterous rumour about you. It was an absurd slander circulated by someone who knew nothing at all about you. The gossip intimated that, although you were a member of the clergy, you had a relationship with a Japanese woman that had gone beyond the bounds of decency. When I heard the rumour, I thought of the pale Japanese woman I had seen at your doorway. But I loathed the attitude of Japanese Christians, who were quick to judge people by appearances, to measure others on mere formalities, and perpetually to regard themselves as righteous. I laughed off the gossip: 'What nonsense!' Because I knew what kind of person, how strong-willed a man you were. I knew at the very least that the man my mother had respected would never do anything like that, even in the worst possible circumstances.

The rumours reached my ears from various sources. Hearsay blended with base curiosity led someone to claim they had seen you riding in your jeep with that woman; another reported that you had been out shopping somewhere with her. I tore into the man who relayed those rumours to me. 'What's wrong with their being in the same jeep? If you've got errands to run, it's all right to be in a jeep with a woman.' He stared into my face with surprise and then blushed. 'She's a divorced woman, you know.' From somewhere he had information about the woman. 'And she has a child.' My mother was a divorced woman, too. A divorced woman with a child. That priest is the one who instilled faith in her, who taught her about a world of greater holiness – the words rose up as far as my throat, but I sealed my lips. For something distasteful, something exceedingly distasteful, had simultaneously welled up in my throat. At that time had my mother been made the object of the same kinds of slanders and rumours by the members of the Church? Had there been gossip that something had happened between her and you? I glared back into the man's face and shouted: 'I don't care what anyone says. I believe in him! I believe in him!'

I believe. It's true that I believed in you. Because you had told me: 'Believe in me.' Even today I have not forgotten what you said to me then, or how your voice had sounded. Do you remember? When, unable to bear the petty rumours any longer, I came to your office to tell you about them. You seemed busy as always. And though you no longer had a scruffy beard, I still sensed some neglect in your dress. I couldn't put my finger on how you were neglectful. Your trousers were pressed, and the evening sunlight streaming through the window splashed against them like a blemish. Yet there was something unkempt about you that I had never detected in the past. I stood directly in front of you and reported that groundless rumours involving you were flying about. You looked up at me with a searching stare. I couldn't tell whether you were listening to what I said or not. When I finished, you were silent for a few moments. I gazed at the stain of sunlight on your trousers. Finally, with vigour, you said: 'Believe in me.'

You spoke the words fervently. Just as when you had said to me in the past, 'Believe in Christ. Believe in God and in His Church', your voice carried the weight of heavy stones and was filled with conviction and confidence. That's how it sounded to me, at any rate. Believe. That Easter Sunday when I was baptized, I had cried out in a loud voice like the other children: 'I believe!' What reason could I have had not to believe? How could I have doubted the man my mother trusted throughout her lifetime? The calm in my heart after I had received the sacrament of penance. A feeling of relief similar to that filled my heart for the first time in many months, and I could not stop myself from smiling wryly. 'Goodbye.' You nodded when I got up from my chair.

There were many complications in my plans to marry the young woman, but I was finally able to persuade my father. However, he had one condition: I was not to get married in one of those 'Amen' churches. How desperately my father wished to sever the psychological tie between me and Mother. I accepted his senseless request, and after I had consulted my fiancée, we decided to have two wedding ceremonies. One would be a ceremony held at a hotel for my father and his friends, the other a service at church with just the two of us. She had by then decided to be baptized. Naturally you were the one who was designated to recite the mass for our ceremony.

The day before our secular ceremony at the hotel, I put on a plain suit that would not arouse my father's suspicion, and she dressed in a suit of the same colour, and we unobtrusively called on your seminary. Just the two of us, with no one else to witness; yet I felt that from the far distance my dead mother was giving her blessing to this wedding. I wanted to boast to Mother: 'If nothing else, I've turned my bride into a believer!' When we reached the front of the seminary, my fiancée took out a pure white handkerchief she had purchased without telling me, and placed it in my breast pocket. On her suit she pinned a cattleya. It was touching. 'Please tell Father we're here,' I instructed her.

I waited outside the chapel. It was a clear day. The Quonset-hut buildings were lined up in array. Their duralumin walls glittered in the sunlight. I thought of my mother, and smiled to myself as I wondered what she might have said had she been able to meet my wife. The young woman who was about to become my wife came walking slowly towards me. Her body reeled slightly. She's really excited about this, I said grinning to myself, and threw away the cigarette that was in my mouth.

'What's up? Did you tell him we're here?'

Her face tight, she said nothing.

'Are you feeling ill?'

'No.'

'Then don't look so ridiculous.'

Still her face was contorted, and she would not speak. Scraping the ground with the toe of her shoe, she suddenly said: 'I want to leave.'

'Why?'

'Why . . .?'

'This is no time to start talking nonsense.'

Her face suddenly collapsed, and she whispered: 'I saw them. I saw them,' she said.

When she pushed open the door to your office to announce our arrival, you were just separating your body from that of the pale woman we had once met at your doorway. Her face had been directly beneath yours, and my fiancée left without a word, leaving the door open.

'What!' Fury pierced my chest. 'That's impossible!' I slapped her across the face with an open palm. 'Are you going to take part in those ridiculous rumours, too?'

She pressed her hand against her cheek. Your words came slowly back to me: 'Believe in me.'

The ceremony. Her eyes were red and swollen from crying. Did you think they were tears of joy? You couldn't have. You couldn't have done anything like that. As I stared at you and at the altar while you performed the mass, I struggled to subdue the doubts that kept welling up in my chest like foul bubbles that rise to the surface of a murky swamp. 'Believe in Christ,' you had told me. There was no way you could recite the mass of Christ if you had just done something like that. Even then I was trying to believe in you.

After we were married, I frequently reproached my wife when her face twisted at the memory of that morning. 'Do you doubt the man my mother trusted more than anyone else?' And my wife would shake her head. But if, in fact, what she told me was true, it meant that the one pure ceremony of marriage she would ever experience had been performed by a priest with filthy hands. That would have been just too cruel. In order to distance myself from such doubts, I began avoiding you. And three months later, I heard the definitive news that you had left the seminary.

How had this happened? I was in a daze. In any case, I had to meet you and get you to tell me everything. The urge to believe in you no matter what others said mingled with a sense of betrayal to strangle my heart. But they told me at the seminary that they did not know your whereabouts. I lost my temper with them, telling them their answer was irresponsible, but there was nothing to be done. Finally, after all manner of inquiries, I learned that you were staying with one of your fellow-countrymen, a Spaniard in the import-export business.

I sent you a letter. But instead of a reply, all I received was a message from a Spaniard claiming to be your friend, asking me to leave you alone for the time being. I felt I could understand why you didn't want to see even me – no, me especially. I could imagine how isolated you felt amidst your shame and humiliation. I eventually gave up the notion of pursuing you.

But the shock I received had in no way subsided. Just what was going on? When exactly had this absurd business started? I knew none of the answers to these questions. Only one image surfaced from the depths of my memory – the scruffy, chestnut-coloured beard that smudged your chin like grime the first time I brought my wife to your office. Had you, by any chance, already begun to decay then? Perhaps something invisible to the eye had already started to gnaw away imperceptibly at your way of life, at your faith. That's what I felt. Of course this amounts to nothing more than my own futile imaginings.

But why did you lie even to me, to one who made every effort to believe in you? In response to my words of caution, you had said in such a confident voice: 'Believe in me.' Anger and pity took turns to stab into my heart, and at times my anger led me to imagine even more fearful things – that you may have deceived me and my mother for a very long time. In every instance I rejected such thoughts, driving them from my mind.

My wife would no longer speak of you. 'I'm not going to church any more. I can't believe in any of it.' I could not formulate any assured retort to her murmurings. 'Are you going to find fault with all of Christianity just because of one missionary?' But I knew all too well that such an answer would not satisfy even my own mind. I was not alone: many clergymen and members, at a loss to explain this unexpected occurrence, felt dazed and lowered their voices to whispers. Ultimately they closed their eyes to the whole affair, burying it beneath the ashes of silence; in other words they adopted the attitude that a lid must be placed over objects that begin to stink.

But I was in a quandary. Unlike others, I could not be satisfied with waiting for the passage of time to cancel out the rumours, or for everything to be obliterated by forgetfulness. For me, forgetting you was the same as forgetting Mother, and rejecting you was to deny the wide river that was my life up until then. Unlike many converts, I had not chosen Christianity of my own volition. For a long while my faith had in a sense been tied to my attachment to Mother and linked to my veneration of you. Those aspects of my faith were being betrayed to their very roots. At this late stage, how could I join the others in forgetting you, in covering over the problem?

So I asked a number of priests: 'Please go and see him.' I wanted to believe (though I still don't know whether it's true) that you had abandoned the seminary and run into the arms of a woman out of a greater faith – an act, perhaps, of even greater love. And I wanted you to prove to me that even now – no, now more than ever – you possessed even stronger faith. But such childish daydreams were soon shattered. Most of the priests rejected my request, which initially angered me. Christ had never visited the fortunate or the fulfilled. They had always told me that He had hurried to the side of those who were alone, those who were subjected to humiliation. Yet it seemed to me that, in the present circumstances, no one would extend a hand to you. But my thinking was shallow. Because when one priest finally did get in touch with you, the answer that came back was the simple phrase, 'He doesn't want to see you.' The priest told me: 'I think it's better for you to leave him in peace for now. Don't you understand how he feels?' I finally realized my own insensitivity and egoism.

And so my lengthy association with you came to an end. When I think back on it, I am aware that over thirty years have passed since you first appeared in my room at the Charity Hospital. Your soporific sermons. Remembering how I was forced to give up my dog. My agony as I ran with you along the mountain path. The incident in the dormitory. Mother's death. Your hands, swollen with frost-bite, giving me your own ration of butter in Karuizawa. Each of those moments was deposited as an essential component in the river of my life. The marks that one person leaves on the life of another. We never realize what sort of marks we leave upon the lives of others, never know what diversions we bring as they pursue their course. Just as the wind twists the shape of a pine tree planted on a sandy beach, changing the angle of its branches, you and Mother, more than anyone else, bent my life in the direction it has taken. And now you have disappeared.

I later heard through the grapevine that you were supporting yourself by becoming an instructor at an English conversation school and teaching private Spanish lessons. Someone told me that a child had been born to you and the Japanese woman. These pieces of news were absorbed into my heart with less of a sense of shock than before, and the incident that had temporarily caused such consternation among the members of the church was gradually passing from memory.

My wife and I have never again mentioned what happened before our wedding ceremony. It's not that the topic never comes up, but that we both avoid touching upon it. And yet, sometimes after we have finished dinner and I move from the kitchen to my study, closing the door tightly behind me and facing my desk; or late at night when I raise my head from a book, I suddenly hear your voice. 'Believe in me.' At such times I struggle to get a hold on you in some way or other in order to sustain my belief in you. That was one of the reasons I made you a character (significantly altered, of course) in three of my novels and tried in various ways to probe your mind. Perhaps, just as you led my mother to a higher plane of existence, you were tripped up in your attempt to elevate the life of that woman with the pallid complexion. At first you didn't realize that your emotions as a man were gradually mingling with your compassion and your feelings as a priest. You had too much confidence in yourself. You didn't know that a mighty tree can snap without warning. Perhaps your excess of self-assurance is what unexpectedly tripped you up. And once you stumbled, the speed with which a man like you slides down the embankment is swift. Many times I made a stab at formulating such hypothetical schemes, and each time I failed. In the final analysis,

I don't understand the truth about your fall. And, yes, it's true that the wounds in my heart were not healed by setting up such suppositions.

But one day I saw you again, for the first time in many years. It was on the roof of a department store one Saturday evening. At the time I was living in Komaba, and sometimes I would take my son to the playground there on the roof. It was one of those days. My first-grade son rode around in a twirling teacup, and became engrossed in a mannequin that talked when you inserted a coin. A large circular contraption with several aeroplanes attached to it whirled to the music as the planes flew through the air. Fathers and mothers sat on a chair here, a bench there, relaxing and watching their children just as I was, and I bought myself a Coke and drank it slowly as I read my newspaper. I glanced up, and there I caught a glimpse of you from behind.

A tall wire fence had been stretched around the edge of the roof to prevent accidents. On this side of the fence were several telescopes that provided a brief view of the city when a 10-yen coin was inserted, and the children brought here by their parents had clustered round them. You were standing by yourself between the telescopes and the fence, looking out at the darkening city. A large bank of leaden clouds spread over the city, and only one slice of sky to the west glimmered a milky white, spilling a few beams of faint, forlorn sunlight. It was an utterly commonplace evening sky for Tokyo, and viewed from my angle your body appeared somewhat shorter than the buildings and apartment houses in the distance. Maybe it was due to the smog, but the lights that had been turned on in some of the windows of the buildings shone with a strange blur, and pieces of underwear and bedding were hanging out to dry outside the apartments. You no longer wore the black cassock and Roman collar of a Catholic clergyman. I think you were wearing a tattered grey suit. It may have been the suit that made me feel that your body, which had been so imposing in the past, had become somehow thin and shabby. It may be rude to use such a description, but you looked to me like some provincial foreigner.

What I found unusual was the fact that I felt no particular surprise. Instead the whole thing seemed natural, something to be expected. I don't know why. The assurance and confidence you once possessed had vanished now, and none of the many ordinary Japanese parents and children who were passing the time on the roof of the department store that evening gave you even a second glance. Almost inadvertently I started to get to my feet. But just then a familiar-looking woman, tugging at the hand of a child dressed in a white knit outfit, came over to you. The two of you turned your backs on me and headed for the distant exit, walking as if you were shielding the child.

I said that I had met you, but that was all there was to it. Of course I said nothing about it to my wife. That negligible reunion has popped into my mind in recent years, often at night. And as I ponder how you looked as you stood with your back to me, that image is superimposed upon several other shadows that have crossed the river of my life. The old White Russian man selling Russian bread in Dalian when I was a child. The elderly foreigner who furtively slipped into the priest's quarters, dragging his tired legs. (That old foreigner was expelled from the priesthood for getting married, just as you were.) One summer twilight, as I tried to run away from him, he had said: 'Don't be afraid of me.' His plaintive eyes overlap with the eyes of the mongrel you made me get rid of. Why is it that the eyes of animals and birds are filled with such sorrow? I can't help but feel that all of these images have formed into a chain inside me, binding themselves together into blood relations, and are trying to communicate something to me. But when I make room for them in my life as a kind of chain, I can no longer think of you as a dynamic missionary brimming with confidence and conviction, nor as a man, standing between lighted buildings and apartment houses where washing hangs out to dry, who looks down on life from a higher position and passes judgement upon it. Instead, I think of you as a man whose eyes are now no different from the sad eyes of a dog. As a result, even if you did betray me, my bitterness over that has diminished. In fact, I even think that the person you once believed in came here for just such a purpose. Or perhaps you already know that. Because in that restaurant at Shibuya, with a drizzling rain falling outside, you quickly and inconspicuously crossed yourself after the waitress delivered your food. That's all I really understand about you now.

A Fifty-year-old Man

'All right , now to the criticisms. Kon-san, when we were doing the waltz, you continued to loosen your grip of your partner.'

'Right.'

'When your grip loosens, you look sloppy. That's what I always say.'

After the group finished dancing, the dance instructor offered criticism to the seven mixed couples as they wiped away their sweat. When this amateur dance group was first formed, renting a classroom at a dressmaking school, a bank employee became their teacher. He was selected because in his college days he had won second place in a nation-wide dance competition.

'Sonny, your rhythm is all off. You still have some bad habits you picked up from cabaret dancing.'

'I understand.'

'Mimi-chan, why is it you turn your face away when you're dancing with Sonny?'

'It's horrible. He had some pot-stickers to eat today before he came here.'

While the others laughed the instructor grinned feebly, and finally he looked towards Chiba and simply remarked: 'Mr Chiba, you still look at your feet from time to time. You need to have more confidence in your steps.'

The teacher called the others in the group by pet names like Kon-san, Mimi-chan or Sonny, but Chiba alone he referred to deferentially as 'Mr Chiba'. Chiba was past fifty, considerably older than anyone else in the dance group.

'That's all for today.'

Everyone pitched in to return the desks and chairs that had been pushed to a corner of the room to their original position, after which they went out into the deserted, dusty-smelling hallway. An inconsequential drizzle was falling outside, but the moisture felt good on their sweat-soaked foreheads. When they reached the road leading to the railway station, the young people turned to head for a bar, but Chiba alone bid them farewell. The young people all bowed to him. He hailed an unoccupied taxi, and when he sank down into the back seat, forgetting even that there was a driver, he muttered to himself: 'Ah, I'm so tired!' It was hard work at his age to dance for an hour and a half without a break, and again today he was stiff from his thighs down to his ankles.

'Is something wrong?' the driver, looking back, asked with concern.

'It's nothing,' Chiba answered vaguely. He was embarrassed to be out dancing at his age. Even his wife gave him a strange look when he announced that he was going to learn to dance in order to tone up his legs, which had become quite frail. Why not golf? she inquired. I don't like golf, it takes up too much time. I wanted to learn how to dance when I was young, but I couldn't because of the war. Just an old man's stubbornness? What are you talking about? I'm not all that old yet. He bluntly brushed aside his wife's suggestion.

'How's business?'

'Not good at all.' The driver shrugged his shoulders. 'Last year, I didn't even have to go out looking for customers, they'd come looking for me. But now all of us drivers are falling over each other to snatch away customers. Do you think times'll get better next year? We don't have a union, see. . . .'

A stabbing pain suddenly pierced the back of Chiba's head. It started just at the point where his hair spun in a whorl, and spread in all directions like black ink poured into a glass of water. Chiba clutched at his knees to combat the pain. After all, taxi driving's nothing more than a job to bring in a day's wages.

In a union, anybody who complains just gets the axe. Why, even in my own case . . .

'I'm sorry, but . . .' Chiba panted, 'I've got a terrible headache.'

'Eh? That's awful.' Quickly the driver proposed: 'Would you like to go to a hospital?'

'No, I'll be fine. It'll go away soon.'

This was not the first time he'd experienced such a headache. They had afflicted him without warning three times since last year. He knew the cause. When he went without sleep or engaged in activities too strenuous for a man his age, his blood pressure would suddenly climb as high as 200. At such times, Chiba was invariably stricken with a migraine.

'Are you sure you're all right?' The driver seemed less concerned than anxious that something tiresome might happen in his taxi. 'Don't you think you ought to go to a hospital?'

'I'm all right.'

When he closed his eyes and controlled his breathing, the intense pain gradually subsided, like a toothache yielding to an analgesic. Afterwards a dull ache that he was able to endure lingered on for about a day. As he leaned his body against the window of the vehicle, it occurred to him that his mother had died of a stroke when she was fifty-four. The first time he'd had his blood pressure taken, the doctor had asked him if any of his relatives had suffered a stroke. And he had been informed many times that this condition was inherited.

'Well, then,' Chiba jested as he always did, 'I won't have to worry about dying of cancer, will I? I'd much rather drop dead of a stroke.'

The night his mother died, Chiba had been out partying. He was still burdened with the knowledge that he had been merry-making in his mother's final hour. When the doctor informed him that his blood pressure was high, he actually felt almost happy that he might be able to die in the same manner as his mother.

Once he passed the age of forty-five, Chiba brought the

laughter of his family upon his head by buying up all kinds of folk remedies and dubious pieces of fitness equipment, all in the name of taking care of his health. He gulped down green potions made from bamboo grass and tea brewed from the Chinese matrimony vine; into his bath-tub he inserted a machine that belched up bubbles; and he installed an electric massage chair in the parlour. He tried walking on stalks of green bamboo, and he even bought a cycling machine at an exorbitant price. He stayed with none of them very long, and ultimately his wife had to carry the massage chair and the bicycle out into the shed in the garden. By now he was reduced to taking dancing lessons to strengthen his legs and back, and taking their dog for a walk each day when he had a few free moments.

Chiba had liked dogs since his childhood. He didn't really know why. Perhaps it was because when he was still at elementary school his dog was the only companion to whom he could admit his own grief over the discord and the talk of divorce between his parents.

At that time, his family was living in Dalian in Manchuria. By the end of September in Dalian, nearly half the leaves had fallen from the trees lining the streets, and each day the sky was filled with grey clouds. At school he would perpetually tell jokes and play the clown, but once class was dismissed and he was left on his own, he never wanted to return straight home. He hated to see his gloomy-faced mother, seated in an unlit room like a stone statue. His elder brother, who was in junior high, would come home from school and without a word sit at his desk and open his books. Even as a boy Chiba had been painfully aware that his brother behaved in this manner in an attempt to endure the discord between his parents. When finally he returned home, he did not go in the front door but would hide his school bag in the shade of the fence and roam endlessly outdoors. At such times, his cross-breed dog would follow him wherever he went.

Kicking up the desiccated acacia leaves, he would stare at the Manchurian children playing with their skipping-ropes, or kill time by going to the pond in the park, still not capped with a thick layer of ice, and throw stones at the old boats tethered to piles. The dog would lie down beside him, staring at some vague point in the distance. When the sun began to set, and his kneecaps, exposed below his short trousers, began to ache from the cold evening air, he still didn't want to go home. It hurt him to listen from his room as his father, just home from work, roughly snapped at his mother, and to hear her sobbing voice.

'I just . . . can't take it any more. . . .' Sometimes he would say that to the dog as it gazed into the distance. Since he always played the fool, he couldn't bring himself to confess the anguish he felt to his teachers or his friends at school.

'I can't take it any more.'

The dog looked at him curiously. But that was enough for him. It was sufficient to have someone to whom he could express his inexpressible sorrow. When he dragged his feet home, the dog would slowly get up and follow a little way behind him, its tail and head bowed.

Finally the day came when his parents decided on a divorce, and his mother gathered her two children to return to Kōbe, where her sister and brother-in-law lived. It was May, when the rows of street-side acacia trees unique to Dalian were in full bloom, their white petals fluttering in the wind and skittering to the pavement. When he climbed into the horse carriage packed with suitcases and wicker trunks, he looked back at the familiar house, only to realize that his dog was standing despondently at the gate looking towards him. When the Manchurian driver gave a lethargic flick of his whip and the carriage jerked forward, the dog chased after it for five or six paces, then stopped in resignation. That was the last he saw of his dog.

The dog had been named Blackie. After he grew up, Chiba always had a dog around the house. Not a Western dog or a dog with a certificate of pedigree, but a mongrel no better than a stray, one that would remind him of his original Blackie, who had stared at him in the Dalian park buried in dead leaves that nightfall in late autumn.

After he got married, Chiba frequently argued with his wife

over his dogs. She had never been fond of animals, and early in their marriage she could not stand having him bring his dog into the house on rainy days, or watching him deliberately leave portions of the food she had gone to the trouble to cook so that he could give them to the dog.

'Try putting yourself in the place of the person who has to do the cleaning around here. I can't stand all the hair it leaves by the door, and all the mess it makes.'

'It's a living thing. It can't help it!' he yelled. 'Even a dog gets cold on rainy nights. Fine. Starting tomorrow, I'll clean the entryway.'

He was, however, unable to stick to his vow longer than two days. His wife criticized him for being wilful in his attachment to the dog, and while this debate continued to rage between them year after year he ended up keeping a mongrel at his house. His current pet, Whitey, he had discovered in a box with his siblings in front of the dairy one spring evening thirteen years ago while he was out taking a walk.

One day late in autumn, while he was working at home, he heard Whitey coughing strangely.

'What do you suppose that cough is?'

'I imagine he has a cold,' his wife answered indifferently. 'He's been doing that for some time now.'

'Why didn't you say anything?'

'Well, why should I say anything just because he's coughing? He's getting old, you know.'

Chiba put on his garden shoes and went out to the doghouse. Whitey was crouched down in front of his aluminium water dish. When he saw his owner, he gave a dutiful wag of his tail, but he also emitted two or three unpleasantly dry hacking coughs. Because some thirteen years had passed since he had acquired this dog, in human terms he was an old man of seventy-five. When Whitey had reached approximately the same age as his owner, every time Chiba came home drunk he would go out into the rear garden and pat the dog's head and encourage him by saying: 'Hey, my friend, we both have our share of problems, don't we?' And when the dog got older, he jested: 'Well, Grandpa, let's keep up the good fight together.' Now the dog had pulled away from him in age and become truly elderly. He lay constantly basking in the sun, and he staggered when he walked; it also seemed he had grown rather deaf, since he would not open his eyes unless you made a fairly loud noise.

'What's the matter?'

As he gently patted the dog's chin, he looked at the pond in his garden. The water, which he did virtually nothing to look after, was a murky black, and a potted lotus plant had finally begun to send its stalks in all directions, displaying brown buds. In the shade of one of those buds, a goldfish lay dead. He had been breeding goldfish in the pond for two or three years. Unlike with the dog, he didn't have to do anything for the fish except feed them occasionally. He thought perhaps some contaminated water had seeped into the pond, but there was no sign that such was the case. Perhaps it had simply lived out its appointed life-span.

Floating belly-up, the stomach of the goldfish was oddly puffy. Its scales, once golden, had turned white, perhaps because two or three days had passed since its death. Chiba suddenly remembered a friend remarking that the only living creature that didn't exude a sense of death was a killifish. Rather than being impressed by the comment, Chiba was struck by how old his friend had grown, so sensitive had he become to the death of inconsequential creatures.

'We're both getting old, aren't we?' He attached the leash to his dog's collar and set out. Whitey could no longer walk at the same nimble pace as when he was young. He faltered a bit, the only sign of energy his agitated breathing, as he slowly ambled ahead of Chiba. From time to time he sniffed at scents along the roadside, halted and urinated a few drops, and then made that loathsome cough.

He took Whitey to the little veterinary clinic where he always got his rabies injections. The young veterinarian had rolled up the sleeves of his sports shirt, and sat in the empty examination-room browsing through a comic book with the drawing of a nude woman on the cover.

'I'd better take a blood sample. He may have filaria again.'

Filaria, which most dogs contract from mosquitoes, was just what Chiba had feared might be the problem. Ordinarily dogs were given an annual vaccination against the disease, but such a potent medication could not be administered to a dog as old as Whitey.

Suddenly hoisted on to the examination table, Whitey gave Chiba a piteous look. He resembled a pathetic old man who's been dragged off to the doctor by his relatives and forced to strip naked. He and the doctor restrained the dog, telling him: 'It's all right, it's all right.' When the doctor poked a needle into his rump, Whitey howled as if to say 'That hurts!'

'He has filaria again after all,' the young doctor mumbled as he peered through his microscope. 'I can't use the strong medicine because of his age. He's really become quite infirm.'

'About how long does a dog usually live?'

'Normally around ten years. So your dog has survived quite a long while. I know one dog who lived to twenty, but he was an indoor pet.'

'Very well, then, I'm going to see to it that Whitey lives twenty years and gets appointed an honorary citizen of this town. You'll recommend him, won't you, doctor?' Chiba threw in his routine jest.

The old dog still looked frightened and pitiful as Chiba led him home, and he remembered the spring day when he had first set eyes on Whitey. A cardboard box had been placed in a sunny spot in front of the dairy, and four puppies peered out from it. As he passed by, Chiba unwittingly stopped and gaped inside. A white ball of wool came crawling towards him, and when he looked at it more closely, one of its eyes, caked with mucus, was clenched shut. Still the one-eyed puppy wagged its tail so furiously it seemed as if it would fly off at any moment.

'You can have one for nothing. Any one you like,' the dairyman called out. 'That one's no good. One of his eyes won't open.'

Chiba smiled. 'That's why I want him. Can I have him?'

And so Chiba took Whitey into his home. Once again his wife looked annoyed, but several doses of liver oil cured the puppy's eye.

'I can't take it any more. It's no good as a watch-dog and it does nothing but make trouble for me.'

Whitey provided a constant source of bickering between husband and wife. It was true that this kind of dog was so friendly it wouldn't bark when a pushy salesman came to the door, but would welcome him with wagging tail. When Chiba took him out for a stroll, he would suddenly stop in front of some stranger's house and drop a load, or he might slip out of his collar and run away and not come back for two or three days. On those occasions, invariably they would receive a complaining telephone call. Someone would protest that Chiba's dog had made strange moves on their foreign-bred hound. Every time they got one of those calls, Chiba repeatedly bowed his head into the receiver apologetically.

'If you're going to have a dog anyway, could you please get one a bit brighter? That idiot dog's of no use to anybody.'

'Are you telling me we ought to get rid of him if he's no use?'

From the garden, Whitey watched dolefully through the glass door as Chiba and his wife bickered. Being the kind of man he was, Chiba was irritated by his wife's contention that something was unbearable because it was of no practical use. Once he had bought a used Austin and driven it. For a couple of years the second-hand car had served him and his wife and family quite well. When they all crammed into the car and tried driving up a hill, the vehicle would wheeze, as though it were panting, even asthmatic.

One day, when his wife proposed, 'Dear, why don't we get rid of this old clunker and buy a new car?', Chiba got truly angry. For some time now he had felt as if that car, which breathlessly climbed the hills transporting his entire family, was the very image of himself. He stubbornly rejected his wife's suggestion, and once again had a row with her.

'Who gives a damn about raising some foreign dog? Isn't that right, Whitey?' When the quarrel was over, Chiba went out into the garden, and just as he had done in Dalian in late autumn, he spoke his heart only to his dog. Whitey lowered his head as though abashed, and licked his master's hand.

'What's someone of your age doing trying to learn ballroom dancing?'

Whenever one of his friends taunted him in this manner, Chiba would jokingly respond: 'Dancing's the only time someone my age can freely put his arms around a young woman.'

At rehearsals, of course, during the two hours or so that they were drilled in the complicated steps of the dance, he never had the leisure to sense the woman in his partner. At those times, Mimi-chan and the other women who danced with him became no more than accessories to the dance, like the music or his patent-leather shoes.

'Mr Chiba, move the lower part of your body in closer. You've got to thrust in right between her legs.'

When the teacher shouted these directions, which might have been taken to mean something different in other circumstances, no one laughed, and not even Chiba thought it strange. Even when Chiba jabbed his thigh between the young woman's legs he felt nothing whatsoever. Once he had finally pounded the complex steps into his head, however, he secretly began to savour the smell of sweat emitted by the body of this woman young enough to be his daughter.

As they waltzed or tangoed, circling the floor of the classroom-cum-ballroom two or three times before the music stopped, a stream of sweat trickled down nineteen-year-old Mimi-chan's neck. Her pulsating flesh blushed a faint red, and he smelled the faint aroma of sweat undiluted by perfume. This was not a neck or chin globbed with flesh and rippled with wrinkles like his wife's; and, making sure the teacher did not notice, he quietly inhaled the smell of the young woman's sweat, and thrilled to a momentary sensation not unlike vertigo. And the thought that always came to him after that attack of dizziness had gone was that he was an old man past the age of fifty.

As he came to feel at home on the dance-floor, he got caught up in a variety of fantasies as he watched the teacher and the others dancing. When the teacher and his partner demonstrated the tango, they shook their heads and bodies violently. That reminded Chiba of the convulsions of intercourse, and the way Mimi-chan tilted her head and stared vacantly off into space when they waltzed together made him think of the look on the faces of young women truly in love. When he danced with a partner who had no interest in him, the way she moved her legs seemed slapdash, and there was a hardness to the way she used her hands. Nearly a year had passed since they had started learning to dance, and Chiba was able to guess from the way the women danced just how much of a sense of intimacy had developed between the various men and women of the group, and the fluctuations of their hearts.

He naturally said nothing about any of this. He kept secret the thoughts that passed through a fifty-year-old man's mind as he inhaled Mimi-chan's sweat. When they had finished dancing, he joined the others in putting the chairs and desks back in place in the classroom, and then walked down the empty hallway and out through the door. When they reached the main road, he bid farewell to the young people who were going off for a drink, and they bowed to him and said goodbye.

As summer approached, Whitey's cough grew worse. The veterinarian, noting that it would have little effect since he couldn't use the more potent injections, gave Chiba some liquid medicine to pour down the dog's throat. Whitey slept beneath the shade of a tree nearly all day long, and once in a while he would get up and stagger over to the pond, where he drank the blackened water and coughed. On the surface of the pond one lotus flower had bloomed in the sultry heat.

One sweltering morning, Chiba was abruptly awakened by his wife.

'Get up! Your brother's in a critical condition!'

From his bed Chiba looked up blearily at his wife's round face. His head was still fuzzy, and the vibrant image of his only brother did not mesh in his mind with the words 'critical condition'. 'What nonsense are you talking?' he quietly mumbled to his wife.

He jammed his feet into his shoes and raced ahead of his wife out into the street. The taxis that ordinarily passed by here with annoying frequency were nowhere to be seen. The broad street that early morning was vacant, and several blue plastic buckets were lined in front of stores still closed for business. The taxi they were finally able to hail somehow seemed to have no speed, and stopped lethargically at every red traffic light. At one of those signals, he remembered that he had been out romping the night his mother collapsed with a stroke, and that he had not been there at the moment she died.

In the hospital corridor, his two nieces were weeping. Through their sobs, they told him that early in the morning their father had suddenly vomited up an enormous quantity of blood, and twice in his room since he was taken to the hospital he had again coughed up a great deal of blood. Blackish blood-stains still blotched the floor of his room here and there. Large graphs of blood soiled the several towels that had been rolled up in a ball and placed under the wash-basin. Two doctors, two nurses and his sister-in-law surrounded his brother's body as if to protect it, and transfusion bags and an oxygen tank flanked the bed. When an elderly doctor realized that the patient's younger brother had arrived, he signalled with his eyes and accompanied Chiba out into the corridor.

'A vein in his oesophagus ruptured,' the doctor explained, pointing to his own throat. A lump had developed on the blood vessels in his oesophagus and, when that ruptured, blood had come gushing out uncontrollably.

'I've inserted an ice-pack in his oesophagus as an emergency measure. But if I keep it there the whole day, the membranes in his oesophagus will be destroyed. I'm eventually going to have to remove the ice-pack.'

'After you remove it . . . what will happen?'

'He will probably . . . vomit up blood again.'

'Then . . . we're looking at surgery?'

'Yes. But very few of these kinds of operations are performed in the entire world. There is one doctor at A. University who performs it, but. . . .' The old doctor looked searchingly into Chiba's eyes. Chiba had a clear grasp of his unspoken meaning. The operation was extremely dangerous; but there was no hope for his brother except through surgery.

'There's no other way?'

'I'm sorry, but there isn't.'

'Then please go ahead. Will the doctor from A. University come?' His brother's son had not yet arrived, so Chiba spoke in his stead. Chiba's nephew worked at a broadcast network in Hamamatsu, and hearing of the crisis he was now hurrying to the hospital. Until he arrived, the responsibility for making this decision rested solely with Chiba.

He stood beside his brother's pillow; rubber tubes and needles had been stabbed into his body. The patient had lost six pints of blood, and his unfocused eyes were trained on the ceiling. He didn't seem to know that his younger brother had come. A nurse repeatedly checked his blood pressure, and the doctor listened to his weakening heart.

Not once had Chiba considered the possibility that his brother, only three years older than himself, might ever be stricken by such an unexpected calamity. He had always thought that his brother, who was his superior in all respects, would likewise live much longer than he. He had no idea how to cope with the fact that this brother was now on the verge of dying. His intelligent, serious-minded brother had attained a considerable position in society, but that meant nothing to Chiba. For him, his brother was the person who had shared in his youthful grief that cold late autumn in Dalian when their parents had become estranged. Unlike Chiba, who had dawdled outside, not wanting to see his mother's grim face as she sat motionless in her room, his brother, he knew, had endured the situation by sitting at his desk and opening his school-books. Once they were separated from their father, the two brothers had endured many trials they could not express to outsiders, but they knew of each other's pain as intimately as if they had been twins. 'I'm not going to let you die,' Chiba muttered to himself, and left the room.

His wife, who had been sitting alone in a hallway chair, came up to him. 'He's in danger,' he reported, 'but they're going to operate. If they don't save him, I'll end up an orphan.'

She gave him a tearful smile and muttered: 'An orphan means a little child. You really don't know anything about how to use words, do you?'

'There's no telling when I'll end up like this.'

'Don't be silly. You're only just over fifty.'

That's true, he nodded, and walked over to the pay telephone at the end of the corridor. Because they'd raced out of the house so early that morning, there were a number of things he had to report to the housekeeper.

'Any problems?'

'Whitey is acting strangely,' the housekeeper reported. 'He just lies there and won't move at all. His breathing is very heavy, too.'

'Did you call the vet? Call him immediately and have him come over. Immediately!'

He went back to his chair and told his wife that Whitey was dying, but she said nothing. 'Whitey's critical, too,' he repeated. 'Did you hear me?'

'So what if he is? Your brother is the important one.'

His brother was important, of course, but for Chiba Whitey was important too. He started to tell his wife that, but checked himself. His wife knew nothing about the mongrel that had stared at him in the park at Dalian so many years before.

Chiba returned home exhausted the next morning. During the eight-hour operation, he had waited in the hospital room with his brother's family, and then taken turns sitting in the bedside chair and dozing off. When he got home he didn't even speak to the housekeeper but went directly out into the garden. Whitey was lying on his side outside the doghouse, his legs outstretched and his eyes open a crack. His abdomen heaved repeatedly and his breathing was laboured. When he saw his master through narrowed eyelids, he made a desperate effort to wag his tail, but he could not stand up.

'It's all right. It's all right.' Chiba stroked the dog's stomach. 'You don't have to wag your tail.'

The single goldfish still floated upside-down, dead in the murky black water of the pond. Its belly, which had turned white, was weirdly swollen. The dead goldfish floating in the water looked very much like Whitey lying on his side.

The veterinarian came. He poked two thick needles into the dog's rump, which was caked with mud, but the animal no longer had the strength to cry out.

'Will he make it?'

'I'm not sure. He's old, after all. You had better resign yourself to the fact that his time has come.'

'Please do whatever you can.'

'Uh-huh,' the young veterinarian equivocated, with no confidence in his answer. 'I'll do everything possible, but. . . .'

After the doctor left, Chiba picked up Whitey so that he could put him down in the shade where a cool breeze blew. In his arms the sick dog was heavy as a stone. After putting the animal in the shade, he opened its mouth with his fingers and tried squirting some milk between the pink gums with a dropper, but the white liquid dribbled uselessly down the dog's whiskers and on to Chiba's knee.

The sun felt hot. An unsightly growth of weeds surrounded the half-opened cosmos blossoms. Chiba crouched for a long while beside his ailing dog. The dog stretched his four legs out horizontally along the ground, and with his eyes open only a crack lay there motionless. As he gazed at the cosmos flowers, Chiba thought of how many people, how many living things he had encountered in his day. But the people with whom he had truly had some connection, and the living things with which he had had a true bond, were few indeed. His dead mother. His elder brother in the hospital. And the cross-breed dog that had watched him in the park. Certainly Whitey, who had lived with him for thirteen years, had been closely tied to his life. The stems of the cosmos fluttered faintly in the wind, and a single greenbottle fly lighted on the dog's chin. By then, Whitey was already dead. His eyes remained open a crack as they had just moments before, but the abdomen that had struggled for breath was at rest, and around his whiskers the milk that Chiba had squirted into the dog's mouth had dried whitely on his whiskers. As his fingers passed over Whitey's eyelids, Chiba wept.

Sensing what had happened, his wife stepped down into the garden and crouched beside him quietly for a few moments. Then she bleakly muttered: 'He died in place of your brother.' Then she plucked several cosmos flowers and laid them on Whitey's head.

At nightfall, after placing sticks of incense and flowers around Whitey's body, they hurried to the hospital. The patient still lay sound asleep behind a transparent vinyl tent, surrounded by oxygen tanks and transfusion bottles, but his breathing was more regular than Chiba had expected. As the old doctor at the bedside put away his stethoscope, he whispered that if Chiba's brother could maintain his present condition until the following evening, there was hope for him. When Chiba heard those words, exhaustion overtook him in an instant, and he sat down in a chair in the corridor. Once again a headache coursed through the back of his head like ink dropped into water. When he closed his eyes, he remembered his wife saying that Whitey had died in his brother's place. I'll make a grave for you in a flower garden, he told Whitey.

Adieu

When I boarded the bullet train bound for Kyoto, I noticed an elderly couple seated across the aisle from me. At Tokyo Station, a woman who might have been their daughter had come with her children to see the elderly couple off. When the train began to move, the two older people energetically waved their hands at their grandchildren, but once the platform had disappeared into the distance, they sat unmoving and silent in their seats.

The two scarcely spoke during the three-hour ride to Kyoto. The husband, who wore glasses, read a newspaper; as the train approached Shizuoka, the woman poured some tea from a thermos into a paper cup and handed it to her husband. Without a word he took the cup, slowly savoured two or three sips, then passed it back to her. She spent a considerable amount of time finishing off the tea he had left. Ah, I thought, this is what an old married couple are like.

The train emerged from a long tunnel, and when the black roof-tiles of Kyoto came into view, the couple got up from their seats. The husband removed a suitcase from the overhead luggage-rack, and his wife walked towards the exit door carrying a paper bag full of souvenirs. I picked up my briefcase, and as I queued up behind them at the exit, without really trying to eavesdrop I overheard the following conversation:

'When was it we visited the Fushimi Inari Shrine?'

'Fifteen years – no, was it twenty years ago?'

'Twenty years? Can it have been that long?'

I have a memory of elderly people, the sort of memory that causes me, each time I recall it, to feel how peculiar human beings are.

In the summer of my second year in Lyon as a foreign student, I moved out of the college dormitory I had been staying in and went looking for a room where I could live on my own. Clutching an address given to me by the student affairs office, I called at a shabby building in an alley not far from the rue de Plat where the dorm was.

There was no lift, and by the time I had climbed the stairs to the fourth floor I was out of breath. Some time in the spring I had developed a nasty cough, and I constantly felt exhausted, as though a lead weight had been strapped to my back. I rang the bell, and after some time the door, which was secured with a chain, was opened, and an elderly woman with worried eyes peeped furtively through the crack. I told her I would like to see the room, and eventually she unfastened the chain.

A foul stench assailed me the moment I stepped into the room. It was not the smell of food, but something like mildew. The old woman questioned me briefly about my nationality and what I was doing in France, and when I told her I was a student at Lyon University, she showed me to the room they had to let.

It had a large bed, an old clothes dresser, a desk and a chair. The window, facing the summer's setting sun, looked out on the alley; at a window across the street a young man in an undershirt was playing a harmonica that he held in one hand. I heard footsteps, and when I turned round, the woman, who had her eyes fixed on me, had been joined by a bald, red-faced old man who leaned on a cane, perhaps because of a bad leg. It was evident at one glance that they were man and wife.

The husband, in a voice that seemed to demand a look of gratitude from me, announced that there were no other houses these days that would rent a room this fine at so low a price. With deliberate forethought he muttered, as if to himself, that they had no need to rent out a room but had finally decided, at the request of the student affairs office of the university, to make the room available. He struck me as the crafty, miserly sort of fellow common in Lyon, but I had to admit that the rent was cheap.

I ended up renting the room. Three days later, I panted and sweated my way up those stairs to the fourth floor, dragging a heavy trunk, and then made several other trips back and forth between the dormitory and their house. By the time I had finished transporting all my belongings, I was so tired I could hardly speak, and I collapsed on to the large bed in the centre of the room. As my weight came down on it, the old bed gave out a lethargic creak.

I can still remember how blisteringly hot that summer was in Lyon. On my way to college, as I crossed a bridge over the Saône River, painful darts of sunlight rebounded into my eyes from the surface of the murky, oil-black water and from the boats moored to its shores. Just looking at the glaring reflections was enough to exhaust me. I realized that I was weary to my very core.

Each time I recall the summer I lived in that house, the first things that come to mind are the sound of the radio the old husband always kept on, and that strange smell. A dank, mouldy smell like old bundles of paper. No sooner had I stepped through the door than it came faintly but quickly to my nose. My room was off to the right of the doorway, separate from the tiny kitchen and bedroom of the old couple; the smell seemed to come from their living area. If there is such a phrase as 'the smell of old age', then that was what it was. It was an odour built up over many long years, as the breath they exhaled and the smells of their bodies mingled with the food they ate. The incense-like smell of human bodies that no longer emitted the sweat of youth. That smell had seeped into all the walls and floors and even the dilapidated furniture of this house.

I made every effort to live there unobtrusively, but I was still occasionally scolded by the hobbling old man. He would complain that I had forgotten to turn off the lights when I went out at night, or that I had awakened him when I closed the front door after returning home late. But if I bought him some bon-

bons or some *marrons glacés* from my meagre allowance, he would do an immediate about-face and become the most affable of souls.

The walls of their kitchen were decorated with several old photographs of the couple. From the yellow, faded photographs I learned that many years earlier they had managed a café in Algiers. In one picture, a thin woman with bobbed hair, wearing the kind of long skirt that was popular in old French films, stood beside a sickly-looking girl in front of a shop with a sign reading *Café de la Paix*. That was the old woman thirty years before, along with their now-deceased daughter. In another, a plump man sat surrounded by customers, raising his glass happily with all the others. That was the old man. When he was in high spirits, he would collar me on my way back from the student cafeteria, and sipping wine he would boast about the grand life the French had enjoyed in Algeria.

'They were a manageable people in those days. But they're no good any more.'

He was talking, of course, about the Algerians.

'We Frenchmen built hospitals for them and taught them how to read and write, but now they've begun to forget what they owe us.'

When I did not reply, he continued: 'If we French hadn't gone there, they'd still be as sickly and destitute and miserable as they were in the old days.'

At such times his wife, with sheepish, sunken eyes, would wordlessly seize the bottle of wine from which he was drinking. She constantly complained that he drank too much. When his bottle was taken away, his face would fall in disappointment, and he would take out a soiled handkerchief and blow his nose loudly.

The old couple remained in the house the greater part of the day. The husband would fall asleep in his bedroom, either listening to his radio or reading the newspaper. With his bad leg, it must have been agonizing for him to climb up and down the stairs to the fourth floor. The wife would go out to mass on Sundays, and in the evenings she went out shopping for food or to run errands, but she always came back quickly. On my way back from classes I often ran into her on one of her shopping trips. She wore black clothing, and, like me, she walked down the deserted alley with her back slightly bent. Once she told me she was on her way to post a letter to her brother in Bordeaux. When I said, 'A tout à l'heure', she gave me a quick, frightened look and replied: 'A tout à l'heure.'

Sometimes, complaining of a headache, the old man would sleep into the afternoon. I was grateful, if only because I didn't have to listen to his radio.

On those days, the old woman would invite me into her kitchen and make me coffee, but in exchange I had to listen patiently to her complaints. Her husband had not done any serious work since the time they lived in Algiers. She had had to make good his gambling debts, and he refused to give up liquor even though his liver was damaged. She would harp on about his faults, all the while gazing with eyes moist as though after a crying spell at the photographs of their days in Algeria. Now and then I would chime in with a 'Tenez' or a 'C'est vrai?', but I was not the least bit interested or concerned.

'My husband can't do anything if I'm not around. He was like that years ago, and he's the same now. If I were to die first, I have no idea what would become of him.' Her sunken eyes were fixed on one spot in space. 'But I'm getting old myself, and I can't always nurse him and look after him . . .'

'He looks fairly strong physically, but does he have a weak constitution?'

'He used to be strong. But recently he's been getting these headaches like today, or has dizzy spells. It's because of his liver. He's never given up his drinking for even a day.'

'Why haven't you taken him to a doctor?'

She shrugged her shoulders brusquely. 'A doctor just soaks up money from people who aren't all that sick.' With that, she hastily collected the coffee-cup I had emptied and left the kitchen.

At night not a sound could be heard along the alley. Often,

lacking the desire to study or the energy to go out and call on friends, I would lie back on my bed, staring absently at the shadows on the ceiling. There in the silence I would sometimes hear a car racing along in the distance. There in the silence that smell seemed much stronger than in the daylight. Not a sound came from the couple's bedroom. Impulsively I wondered if the old man and woman still slept in the same bed. I was certain the smell would be even more overpowering in their bedroom. I began to feel as if the incense-like smell had permeated my own body since I had moved into this room.

One night as I lay stretched out on my bed gazing at the ceiling, I heard soft whispers and a voice convulsed with sobs coming from the kitchen.

I listened intently. It was the old man whispering, and the weeping voice belonged to the old woman. My response was one of puzzlement: could it be that wives were still driven to tears after a couple have been together this long? Did people continue to cry even after they were old enough to know the futility of weeping about the vicissitudes of life? The thought filled me with sorrow. In the silence of the night, the sobbing seemed as if it would go on for ever. I began to worry that the old woman might have become ill. There was no one else in the house but this old couple and me, and I persuaded myself that I couldn't just ignore the situation.

When I knocked on the kitchen door, the moaning stopped. The old man opened the door and looked up at me in embarrassment. The old woman had both hands over her face, and her shoulders quivered.

'It's nothing,' the old man told me. 'It's just an attack. She has them sometimes. Over our daughter who died. Crying doesn't do any good . . . it won't bring her back to life. . . .'

Still, he slowly stroked his wife's back. When her sobs subsided a bit, she wiped her eyes with a corner of her handkerchief and said: 'Bernard, I'm sorry.'

'Is your daughter the child in those pictures?' I took another look at the old photograph of the young girl in school uniform standing beside her mother in Algeria. The slender girl with bobbed hair squinted in the bright African sun. She looked perhaps seven or eight years old.

'Yes. She died of a fever. My wife wore herself out caring for the girl, and lost all will to live, and I thought maybe if I brought her back to Lyon . . .'

'No, she's lucky to have died so young.' She shook her head firmly. 'She was so sickly, if we'd died first there would have been no one to look after her. . . .'

After I went back to my room, I continued to hear the muffled conversation of the old couple from the kitchen.

It isn't, however, such trivial incidents that I remember about that aged couple. It's something quite different.

The old man was still tormented by severe headaches around the time my summer holiday ended. He would bury his head in both hands and even give out muffled moans. On my way to school one day, I said to the old woman: 'I really think you ought to call a doctor.'

'Yes, yes.' She shrugged her shoulders. 'He gets these headaches because he drinks too much, even though I tell him not to.'

She never said whether she would call a doctor or not. Just as in Japan, there were many older people in France who disliked doctors, so there was nothing further I could or did say to her.

When I came back in the afternoon, his headache had not gone away. The old woman made him some herbal tea, but of course it had no effect on his condition. When I repeated my suggestion with more insistence, she finally agreed with much reluctance to summon a doctor. I went to a nearby clinic with the message.

Before long, a young man carrying a black bag arrived. He disappeared into the old man's bedroom, and for a long while he examined the patient. He asked the old woman for a cup to take a urine sample.

On his way out, the doctor pushed up his glasses and said to me at the door: 'I'll write out a prescription for him. Pick it up at the pharmacy later.'

I asked him what was wrong with the old man.

'His blood pressure is very high . . . and his kidneys are in terrible shape.'

I was able to guess at the meaning of 'blood pressure', but at that time I didn't know the French word for 'kidney'. I had him write the word on a piece of paper, and later I looked it up in a dictionary.

'He'll have to watch what he eats. He should avoid anything greasy or spicy, and cut down on pepper and salt. If he doesn't, he'll continue to have these headaches, and eventually it'll kill him.'

'Kill him?'

'The blood-vessels in his brain will burst.'

'Did you tell all of this to Madame?'

'Naturally.'

He repeated his instructions to me to pick up the prescription at the pharmacy, and then with his black bag flapping against his leg, he went down the stairs.

I took the prescription to the appointed pharmacy, and brought back bottles of white and blue pills, which I handed over to the old woman. He was to take the round white pills before breakfast; the blue medication he was to have without fail after every meal.

The following day the old man's headache seemed to have abated, perhaps because the doctor's visit had comforted him. Throughout the day he listened to the radio, read the newspaper and paced around the house with his cane like an animal in a cage.

But from that day, I slowly became aware of something peculiar. The odour that had filled the house like a layer of invisible dust changed. Each time I returned to the house and opened the door, my nose was greeted by the smells of lard and cooking oil. I had no idea what the old couple had eaten up until that time, but I do know that I had never smelled so strong a smell of lard. With the restrained sort of life they led, I'm sure their daily fare consisted of rather bland foods.

At first I thought nothing of the change. But I had grown so accustomed to the mouldy smell of their bodies in the time I had lived with them that the abrupt change struck me as curious.

In the kitchen one day, I said to the old man as he read his newspaper: 'Does it smell sort of oily in here to you?'

His wife, who was knitting in a chair beside him, sternly responded for him. 'My husband has a bad liver. He has to have proper nourishment.'

'The doctor said he shouldn't eat anything too irritating . . .'

'Yes. I'm very careful about that. I don't let him drink wine any more. There's nothing as irritating as alcohol.'

Her voice was unusually overpowering, so I said nothing more. It wasn't as if I was their son, or even a member of their family. I was merely a boarder. I didn't want to stick my nose in where it didn't belong.

The smells of lard and cooking oil hovered indistinctly in every corner of the house after that. I recognized the fault in the dietary treatment that the old woman was administering, but I couldn't bring myself to reprimand her for her ignorance. Elderly people always think that their own way of doing things is correct.

And so for some time I attributed it all to her stupidity. But I wonder if her lack of knowledge was really to blame.

I can still remember that Sunday in October. It was a bright autumn day, and when I opened my window, laughing children were playing in the stone-paved alley strewn with fallen yellow leaves. The chimes of the church announcing mass echoed from the distance. The old woman set out for mass, while her husband and I remained in the house.

There was a sudden groan of pain from the kitchen. I rushed in to find the old man with his elbows pressed on the table, clutching his head between his fists.

'The pain has come again. That horrible pain.'

His face was flushed red, and the blue veins pulsated through the few strands of white hair left on his nearly bald head. In front of him was a glass with traces of something the colour of lipstick. I knew in a moment that he had downed a glass of cooking wine while his wife was out of the house. 'I'll be all right in a minute.' He forced his lips into an embarrassed smile. 'But would you put away that bottle of wine on the floor? Into the cupboard. If not, she'll find me out.'

I picked up the bottle and opened the cupboard. Next to the olive oil and ketchup I noticed two smaller bottles. Bottles that I had seen before. They were filled with white pills and blue pills. The ones the doctor had instructed me to pick up at the pharmacy. Not one pill was missing. The old woman had not given any of them to her husband.

I can't properly describe how I felt at that moment. With the sort of horror a child experiences when it has its first glimpse of some ghastly insect, I stood at the open cupboard, staring vacantly at the medicine bottles.

'What's wrong? Just put it in there.' His instructions brought me out of my reverie.

Eventually his wife returned. Dressed in black and carrying a handbag, she saw her ailing husband from the doorway and cried out in a quavering voice: 'Bernard!'

After he had fallen asleep in his bedroom, the old woman, with moist eyes, came to my room and complained: 'While I was out he drank some wine. Yes, I know all about it. No matter how often I tell him to stop, he won't listen to me. He's always been like that. He can't get along without me. I can't imagine what would happen to him if I died first.'

As I listened to her lamentations, I suddenly thought of the two pill bottles in the cupboard. I had no idea why she had not given her husband his medicine. She had no reason to detest the old man. I had seen her caring for him each day, and I couldn't believe that there was anything false in her tears as she muttered her complaints. And yet she had fed her husband the oily foods his doctor had prohibited, and she had made no attempt to give him his medication. Her behaviour seemed calculated to bring her husband one step closer to death each day.

Towards the end of autumn, I moved to different lodgings. The new house was owned by a couple who taught at primary school. The day I moved from the old couple's room, the old man remained in bed with a headache and numbness in his hands and feet. At the doorway the old woman held her hand out to me. When I took it in mine, she gazed at me with those worried eyes and whispered 'Adieu'. I wondered whether I should take her meaning as 'farewell', or as literally signifying 'in the next world'. I lowered my head in silence and went down the stairs.

Heading Home

The summer sun was ablaze the afternoon I ordered a new headstone at the mason's in Fuchū.

Just two weeks earlier my brother had died, and we made arrangements to have his ashes placed in the same grave as my mother at the Catholic cemetery in Fuchū. We decided to take this opportunity to enlarge her grave, which was far too small in the first place.

'You realize', the owner of the stonemason's said as he scratched the plump forearm exposed by his short-sleeved shirt, 'we'll have to dig up your mother's body.'

When my mother passed away over thirty years ago, cremation was not permitted by the Catholic Church to which she belonged. As a result, her corpse had been placed in a casket and transported to the Catholic cemetery. Her coffin had been lowered into a dark hole dug by a workman, and my brother and I had sprinkled earth over it. I was still at school at the time, and my brother wasn't well off either, so we couldn't provide her with anything better than a tiny grave. Now my brother was dead, and his family and I had agreed to enlarge her grave and place the urn containing my brother's ashes in with her.

'When you say "dig up", what will happen to the body?'

'Since she was interred, the body will initially be turned over to the police. Then it'll be burned at the crematorium. After that, if you'd be good enough to take charge of the deceased until the new grave is finished. . . .'

I was afraid. After more than thirty years, my mother's body was going to emerge from beneath the ground. It frightened me to think of seeing her reduced to a pile of bones. It wasn't quite the same as Lazarus being restored to life from the grave, but I could almost feel my mother rising up and coming forth in the light of day to point a finger at me and accuse me of living a life of feeble devotion now, just as in the past.

Hesitantly I made my way home beneath the glaring sun. My wife and her cousin, Mitsuko, were eating water-melon in the kitchen.

'You've really lost weight.' Oblivious to my wife's disapproving glance, her cousin unhesitatingly scanned my body and blurted out her concern. My wife hurriedly changed the topic.

'What's happening with the grave?'

In subdued tones I explained that I had ordered the headstone, but that my mother's body was going to be exhumed. 'She has to be burned at the crematorium.'

'So in the Catholic Church you bury the body, do you? I didn't know that,' Mitsuko said with a touch of derision. 'Why is that?'

'Because of the resurrection. But they've changed the policy now, so it's all right to be cremated.'

At the word 'resurrection' Mitsuko peered at me as though she were examining some counterfeit goods. If Mother were here, I thought, she would resolutely proclaim her own cherished beliefs about the resurrection; I realized that I could not do the same.

'Oh.' Again my wife changed the subject. 'Mitsuko has a favour to ask. She wants you to steal a dog.'

'Steal a dog?' I blustered. 'Me . . .?'

'That's right,' Mitsuko said nonchalantly. 'It's a really pitiful dog.'

Near her home, she reported, lived a plasterer whose wife had died. He had a bad drinking problem, and every night he beat the dog that had belonged to his wife. The dog was chained up all day long, and the owner never took it for walks and scarcely fed it. Consequently it howled every night, but each time it did, he would pummel it again.

'It's so pathetic. I've taken food over to it two or three times. He's so cruel – he orders it to miaow like a cat, and when it can't, he beats the poor thing.'

'Hasn't anybody complained to him?'

'Of course we have. But he just threatens us back.'

'But why do *I* have to steal this dog?'

'Come on now, didn't you lose a dog last year? You've still got the doghouse, and both of you love dogs. What? My house? Don't be ridiculous. We live in the same neighbourhood, and he'd know right away that we'd stolen his dog. And besides, we've got two cats.'

She was quite right: there before our eyes in the garden a doghouse stood alone and forlorn. Our old dog had slept there until he turned fourteen (I understand that fourteen years for a dog is like eighty for a human), but then one day while napping beneath the cosmos flowers he died of decrepitude and an infestation of filaria. I buried him in the garden and planted some white magnolia seedlings on his grave.

'I really hate to ask you, but . . . couldn't you keep this poor dog in your doghouse?' She assumed a humble posture as she shifted her eyes towards the doghouse with its peeling paint. It occurred to me that, had my mother been here, she would have refused outright to take care of the dog.

'Well, but to steal the animal . . .'

'Don't worry. Another neighbour and I will take care of the abduction. All you have to do is drive the dog away in your car.'

'What'll you do if you get caught?'

'We won't get caught!'

My wife and I were ultimately railroaded into the plot; it was my timid resolve and my voracious curiosity that finally made me agree to Mitsuko's high-handed proposal.

'I suppose we ought to help this dog out in memory of my late brother.' I said this to my wife to help rationalize the idea to myself, but in fact I couldn't help feeling there was some kind of contradiction in stealing another man's dog as a memorial to the soul of my Catholic brother.

One evening, three or four days later, Mitsuko phoned to

announce that tonight was the night. After dinner, my wife drove us to Isehara, located about forty minutes from our house on the freeway. Mitsuko continued to live in Isehara after the death of her husband, and she taught tea ceremony lessons there. I spread newspapers all over the car just in case the dog happened to throw up, and I also brought along a large *furoshiki*, some dog food and a flask of whisky. The whisky was to bolster my nerve; the *furoshiki* I brought to toss over the dog in case somebody discovered us.

'About their digging up my mother. . . .' Peering at my wife's back while she raced the car along the Tōmei highway, I broached the subject once again. 'Do you think I ought to be there when they do it?'

She said nothing for a few moments, but then quietly responded: 'You're afraid, aren't you?'

I didn't answer. I was of course afraid, but it was more than that. Gazing upon my mother after she had been reduced to mere bones seemed like an act of desecration towards her. My mother herself would surely not want to expose herself so openly to her son's gaze.

'Would you rather I went?'

'No, I must do it. I've got to go to Kyushu the day after tomorrow, but when I get back, I'll call the stonemason's.'

Before my eyes floated an image of the interior of an imperial tumulus that had been laid open by excavation. I had seen photographs of such a place in some magazine, depicting skeletons half buried beneath the ground, their arms and legs partly twisted out of shape. Is that how my mother would reappear from under the earth? My late brother and I knew better than anyone else the agonies she had endured during her lifetime. We were most aware of the strong faith she had maintained. I had no desire to see her reduced to a skeleton from which all agony, all faith, all life had been stripped away.

When we reached Mitsuko's house in Isehara, she and her co-conspirator were waiting for us. They wore hats that looked like mountain-climbing caps, had slipped on men's trousers, and had even remembered to put gloves on. I couldn't imagine why it was necessary to dress up like a student demonstrator or a housewife ready for spring-cleaning just to steal one measly dog. The two women climbed into our car and we drove a short distance. Near the plasterer's house, the second woman got out of the car and went ahead to reconnoitre; she soon came back panting to announce in hushed tones that the dog's owner was not at home. As a man I couldn't very well refuse to help, so I took a gulp of whisky and set off after them. The street was silent, and the little shack where the plasterer lived was dark and abandoned. Mitsuko's accomplice boldly manoeuvred her plump body through a gap in the splintered hedge, and in the darkness we heard the dog snort and a chain rattle. She attached the rope she had brought to the dog's collar, then handed the end to me through a gap in the hedge.

'Pull him through quickly, please.'

'He won't come out. Come on, you beast!' The frightened cur refused to budge. 'Come out, damn you!'

'Hey, keep your voice down!'

My hands were covered with spiders' webs, but I finally managed to drag the scrawny dog through the hedge, his tail between his legs and his head extended as though it were to be lopped off. Mitsuko stroked his head and spoke to him in sweet coaxing tones: 'You poor little thing. Nobody's going to beat you any more.'

I knew her words were directed at me, not at the dog. But we didn't have time to stand around chatting; we thrust the animal into the car and hurried away. The two dog-nappers, still breathing heavily, launched into a lively assessment of their own noble deed. We let them off at a brightly lit street-corner, and my wife and I quickly escaped back to the Tōmei highway. As I gulped down some more whisky, I reached one hand out to touch the dog: he was damp, emaciated and trembling.

When I went out into the garden the following morning, the dog stood looking up at me with timid eyes in front of the doghouse where my dead pet had once resided. He must have been quite hungry, though: when I gave him some dog food, he gobbled it all up, scooting the aluminium dish around with his snout. He had a contusion on his forehead that could have been a scar left from a beating by his former owner.

With no time to fuss over this dog, I set out for Kyushu to gather materials for a book. Catholic missionaries had established a seminary on the Shimabara peninsula at the end of the sixteenth century, and for some time now I had been interested in several of the Japanese who graduated from there. One of them, named Miguel Nishida, had fled Japan during the Christian persecutions and settled in the Philippines, where he laboured as an evangelist in the Japanese community. Eventually he returned to Japan and died here. A letter written by Miguel Nishida had recently turned up in Kyushu, and I wanted to have a look at it.

The sun glared brightly in Nagasaki on the day I met Mr Ōtsuji, the reporter for Nagasaki Broadcasting who had informed me about the letter. He was an old acquaintance who had done me several favours over the years.

'The letter was found by an old established family named Matsuno in Hirado. Professor J from Sophia University and Father P from here in Nagasaki have already come to examine it.'

Mr Ōtsuji took me to a *sushi* shop next to his office, and no sooner had we taken our seats than he pulled an envelope from his pocket. It contained two pages photocopied from the letter. Even in this reproduced form, it was evident that the edges of the paper were worm-eaten. I was able to decipher the first few words: 'I have wanted to write you. All is well here.' But I couldn't make out what followed. Wiping the beer foam from my lips with my hand I pondered the text, until Mr Ōtsuji came to my aid: ' "Although I would like to return to Japan, I know it is a dream that will never be realized . . ." '

'So apparently this is a letter that Miguel Nishida wrote before he was able to come back to Japan.'

'That's right.' Mr Ōtsuji nodded. 'Father P estimates that it must have been written about 1630. Nishida smuggled himself into Nokonoshima in 1631. Have you been to Nokonoshima?'

'Yes, I have.'

I had paid one visit to the tiny island in Hakata Bay. It was in the spring, and the island was jammed with sightseers come to see the cherry blossoms; the pebble-strewn beach was littered with empty cans and discarded lunch-boxes. Miguel Nishida had boarded a Chinese junk from the Philippines and come ashore on Nokonoshima in the dead of night. From there he went into hiding in Nagasaki, but he was betrayed by secret informants among the apostates. Braving a violent storm, he fled on foot, but he ultimately collapsed in the mountains above Mogi and died.

As he ate his lunch, Mr Ōtsuji asked: 'Will you be writing about him next year?'

'I'm not sure. There isn't much material to go on.'

'What would your theme be?'

'There are several I'm considering. . . .' Hedging in my reply, I stared at the frothy beer in my mug. 'I'm stymied about why Miguel Nishida came back to Japan. He knew if he returned that one day he'd be captured and killed, but still he came back in search of a place to die. And he's not the only one. There are many such cases among the Christians who were exiled overseas. I find it hard to understand.'

Mr Ōtsuji stood up abruptly. 'Would you like to go and see the mountain at Mogi where Miguel Nishida died?'

Near Shian Bridge that afternoon the sun shone as fiercely as the flames from a blast-furnace, and the streets were crowded with people and cars. Mr Ōtsuji drove his Corolla up the mountainside. When I first visited here over a decade ago, not many homes had been built in the hills, but each time I returned the number of new buildings had increased. From the top of the mountain there was a splendid view of the bay and the tiny fishing port of Mogi. This land was presented to the Jesuits in the sixteenth century by the Christian war-lord, Ōmura Sumitada. Though few people are aware of the fact, this was the first foreign settlement in Japan.

'When we were children, we used to climb up over this mountain, wiping the sweat from our faces as we made our way through the groves of loquats, to go swimming at Mogi.'

There were many fields of loquats in Mogi. Seen through the car window, the leaves of the loquat trees that were planted in terraced orchards glistened like oil in the ruthless sunlight.

'I wonder if Nishida was trying to escape by boat from Mogi to some place like Amakusa?'

The harbour shimmered like a field of needles, while two fishing-boats floated peacefully in the offing. The Shimabara peninsula rose hazily on the horizon. A tempest had raged as Miguel Nishida hurried through these mountains. There's no way of telling where he was hoping to hide himself as he scaled this mountain. He knew in the end that he would be apprehended, no matter to what corner of Japan he fled. Although he could have lived in peace, surrounded by people who loved him, had he remained in the Philippines, he chose to come back to Japan to die.

Mr Ōtsuji pointed to a road that lay dark beneath the shadows of the loquat trees. 'That road hasn't changed over the centuries. It's the same road Nishida ran along.'

It occurred to me that I would have no advance knowledge of the place where I would breathe my last, though it had probably already been predetermined. But I would inevitably make my way to that spot.

The next day I travelled around the Shimabara peninsula, and I returned to Tokyo sunburned and bathed in sweat. When the taxi from the airport dropped me at home, the doghouse was missing from my garden.

'Where's the dog?' I asked my wife as I handed her my briefcase in the entranceway.

She clutched the bag to her chest and said: 'It . . . ran away.'

'Ran away?'

'The night you left for Nagasaki. It got loose from the rope and disappeared. We looked everywhere for it.'

'Did you tell Mitsuko?'

'Yes. She's really upset.'

I'm fond of any kind of dog, especially a mutt. But somehow I hadn't been able to take a liking to that grovelling dog. Maybe it sensed how I felt and that's why it ran away.

Four days later, we had a phone call from Mitsuko. The missing dog had returned to the plasterer's house. The owner continued to keep the dog chained up all day, and beat it every time he got drunk.

'Why in the world did it go back there?' my wife wondered out loud. 'How did it know its way back?'

Even knowing it would be tormented there, the dog had spent four days searching for its former master's house. And Miguel Nishida, fully aware of the persecution that awaited him, had left the Philippines and made the arduous journey back to Japan in order to die. Once again I could see the old, narrow road blackly shaded by the branches of the loquat trees.

I sat alone in the waiting-room at the Catholic cemetery. From the window I could see a plot of land about 1800 metres square, with stone and wooden crosses arranged in tidy rows, and in the centre a *pietà* of the Virgin Mary. Some of the crosses marked the graves of foreign priests and nuns who had come from distant lands and died in Japan. Passages from the Bible or Latin prayers were engraved on each of the headstones.

It was about eleven in the morning, and the light from the white disc of the sun was beginning to intensify. I could see the workman hired by the stonemason's dressed in dirty trousers and an undershirt, as he industriously drove his spade into the ground. The earth in the cemetery plot must have been soft, for the lower half of his body disappeared beneath ground level much quicker than I thought it would.

I had been unable to summon up the courage to stand beside the grave as he dug. It seemed unlikely that I could endure the moment when my mother's skeleton appeared at the bottom of the widening hole. So while the workman laboured away, I sat on a chair in the waiting-room, with sunlight as dazzling as molten tin pouring through the window. A grey funeral urn and a set of chopsticks had been placed in front of me, and the blinding sunlight shone upon them as well. As I stared at these implements, I suddenly recalled that only two weeks earlier I had used the same sort of chopsticks to transfer my brother's bones from the crematory furnace into a similar urn. His bones were so small and scattered that it was impossible to tell from which part of his body they had come; some were a milky white colour, while others had taken on a brownish tinge from being somewhat scorched. 'Erue, Domine, animam ejus. Requiescat in pace. Amen.' Beside me, the priest had intoned the prayer in hushed tones. As my wife and I latched on to the same bone with our chopsticks and lifted it into the urn, the realization that I was now the sole survivor in my family surged in my chest.

While he was still alive, my brother stood between me and death, but now he was gone, and I felt as though death loomed like a black barricade on the path ahead of me. My parents had separated when I was still a child, so I had clung all too tenaciously to my mother and brother to the exclusion of all others. With both of them dead now, I felt truly alone and forsaken.

When I looked out of the window again, the workman's movements had slowed. Finally he thrust his spade into the mound of dirt and painstakingly wiped the sweat from his face with a cloth. Then he turned away, his powerful shoulders glistening, and with a large sieve in his hand he climbed back into the hole. I realized from his movements that my mother's skeleton had appeared from under the ground, and that he was going to collect the bones. 'May she rest in peace.' The prayer erupted from my lips. Resting both hands on my knees, I recited the same prayer that had been offered when I gathered my brother's bones.

Five minutes passed. Ten minutes. Finally the workman stood up in the hole and put the sieve beside his spade. He climbed from the hole and, shielding his eyes against the sun, looked towards the waiting-room. Then he slowly walked towards me. 'I've finished,' he announced curtly. 'Please bring the urn.'

The sun pounded against my forehead. I walked behind the workman, threading my way between one cross and another until we came to my mother's grave. The sieve rested on the mound of earth, and at the bottom of it were clumps of what looked like rotted splinters of wood. I caught my breath. This was what remained of the mother we had buried over thirty years before.

'I'm . . . sorry.'

Taking my words as an expression of gratitude to him, the workman brusquely replied: 'You're welcome.' I'm . . . sorry – inwardly I repeated the words to the bones. Reduced now to a cluster of something resembling decayed chips of wood buried in the mud, hers were so unlike the fresh, milky-white bones of my brother at the crematorium. Was this single pitiful skeleton all that remained on earth of my mother's life, my mother's faith? When I picked up one of the bones with the chopsticks and dropped it into the urn, it rattled feebly. The workman put both hands on the spade he had thrust into the heap of earth and waited attentively for me to finish my work.

'Have you almost finished?'

When I nodded and stood up, I felt a little dizzy and my knees wobbled. From atop the mound of earth I peered down for a few moments into the dark hole that was like an old well. My mother had been interred in this pit for over three decades. Soon the urn containing my brother's bones would also be placed there.

I wrapped the urn in a white cloth, and the workman and I went to the stonemason's near the cemetery. The owner there had agreed to drive me to the crematorium.

The owner was still out on an errand, so I sat down on a rock in his compound to wait for his return. Granite headstones, votive lanterns and statues of the guardian deity Jizō sur-rounded me. The urn I held on my lap now seemed quite a bit heavier than my brother's. As I gazed up at the sweltering white sky, I wondered how the bones of my mother, who had been so short and petite, could be so heavy. Surely it was a result of the partiality and attachment I continued to feel towards her even now. Mother had not necessarily treated me with gentleness. In fact, being as indolent and dilatory as I was, the fervour of her solitary life and faith had caused me no end of torment. During my school-days, unable to endure her any longer, I had even run away and moved in with my father, whom she had divorced. But while I lived with him I continued to feel guilty for abandoning Mother.

'In the end, I'll be buried here with you as well,' I muttered to the urn on my lap. I recalled the deep, round, dark hole I had just seen, and realized that it would be the spot where I would live eternally with my mother and brother.

A car drove up, and the owner of the stonemason's returned.

'You brought the permission form from the police, didn't you?'

It was necessary to have permission from the police to exhume a body. Without such a document, the crematorium would not incinerate the remains.

'Yes, I did.'

Before we got in the car, he commented as though he had just recalled: 'The tombstone is ready. Would you like to see it?'

He took me to his workroom behind the rows of lanterns, and there he gave an order to two young men with towels wound about their heads. They carried out a brand-new, blackly glistening headstone and placed it on the ground. This would be erected beside the new grave.

My mother's name and her date of death had been carved on the right-hand side of the stone. Next to that were engraved my brother's name and death date. Fondly I gazed at the two names, and then realized that a large empty space had been left beside them. Yes . . . next to theirs, one day my name will be etched.

Japanese in Warsaw

That evening large, fleecy clouds danced over the Warsaw airport. About ten Japanese disembarked from the Polish Airlines flight that had just landed. Compared with the Poles on the flight, who wore fur hats and were fully braced against the winter cold, the company of Japanese stood out conspicuously with their shoulders frigidly hunched, cameras dangling from their necks, and the Japan Airlines bags with their distinctive crane designs. They clustered together by themselves at the back of the queue waiting to pass through immigration, nervously holding out their passports.

Suddenly, from amongst the throng gathered to welcome the arrivals, a young Japanese man wearing a ski-cap and woollen gloves called out: 'Are you with Mr Tamura's party? I'm Shimizu, of the Orbis Travel Bureau. I'm here to meet you.'

'Hey, somebody's come to meet us,' one of the Japanese yelled out.

The other foreigners turned round in surprise at the loudness of his voice.

'What a relief! We'd have been goners for sure if somebody wasn't here to meet us.'

'How strict are the Customs people here?'

'They're very strict when it comes to declaring how much money you're bringing in, but at Customs they'll probably search only one of you.'

After they passed through immigration, Shimizu led the Japanese group *en masse* to Customs, where they began unlocking their luggage. The Customs agent, wearing a uniform re-sembling that of a policeman, extracted a tin of dried seaweed from one suitcase and asked in English what it was. The Japanese man gestured with both hands to suggest that he was eating, and answered: 'Ea-to. Ea-to.' After Shimizu explained in Polish, the agent drew a circle with white chalk on the suitcase. When the Customs inspection was finished, the Japanese walked to the rented coach that was waiting for them outside in the cold.

In the faint light of dusk, as they raced along the motorway leading directly into the city, the scene that stretched out before their eyes through the windows on one side of the bus was of a vast expanse of snow splotched with dark-purple shadows. Far in the distance, beneath a gloomy sky, the city of Warsaw looked frigid and forlorn.

'This is really depressing. It's very different from Paris, Mr Shimizu.'

'Warsaw was brutally damaged during the war.' Shimizu answered dutifully, not even turning round in his seat near the driver. He didn't seem to feel a jot of intimacy or fondness towards his fellow-countrymen.

'How many years have you lived here?' Tamura asked.

'Two years.'

'Is this a part-time job? Are you a student?'

'Yes, I am.'

As the coach pulled into Warsaw, tired-looking men and women wearing fur hats were hurrying home from work along pavements sullied with mud and snow. There was a screeching noise when a run-down tram turned the corner. A long queue of people waited patiently at the tram-stop.

'It's desolate. There's hardly a neon sign anywhere.'

'This is Saski Plaza,' Shimizu reported without expression. 'Your hotel, the Europejski, is on this plaza.'

The coach slowly circled the darkened square. It stopped in front of a dilapidated, nineteenth-century-style building that looked imposing only on the exterior, and two porters from the hotel, dressed in gold-braided uniforms, came out to welcome them.

'I'll handle all the arrangements, so please let me have your passports. It will take some time to complete the paperwork, so please take a seat in the lobby.' Standing in front of the revolving door at the hotel entrance, Shimizu collected passports from each of the ten Japanese as they got off the coach, then went alone to the front desk to arrange the room allocations.

'We shouldn't have come here.' The Japanese sat down and looked anxiously around the dimly lit, deserted lobby, which had nothing more to offer than an inordinately high ceiling. The only sound from the front desk was the tapping of typewriter keys. Two or three of the men went to have a look at the gift shop in the far corner, but they came back with sneers on their faces.

'No good. No good. Nothing worth buying. I have no idea what kind of souvenirs to get from this place.'

'Women. This is one of those great places for women nobody knows about.' Tamura, who seemed to be the leader of the group, sought to encourage his downcast comrades. 'That's why we came here. Isn't that right, Imamiya?'

Imamiya was flicking the Dupont lighter he had bought in Paris, while his eyes followed two young women who had just come into the hotel. Both women were tall and blonde. The men had come here because they had heard there were many beautiful women in Poland, and the sight of these two confirmed that report. During this foreign excursion Imamiya had paid for women in London and Paris, but none of them were to his satisfaction. As co-workers in the same industry these men had travelled overseas on the pretext of observing factory operations, but Imamiya, like the other Japanese, had conjured up private goals unrelated to factory observation: to buy a lot of things and to dally with a lot of women.

Once the rooms were assigned and the keys handed over, the group climbed to the second floor and turned the knobs of the doors to the rooms where they would be staying in groups of two. Each room was so dismal, with a hard bed and a torn shade on the bedside light, that they wondered if this was truly a first-class hotel for Warsaw. The wash-basin in the bathroom was black with grime, and the drain in the tub was revoltingly rusted. When they turned on the hot water to test it, it came out a murky red colour, obviously not something they wanted to use. Imamiya, who had teamed up with Tamura, noticed with alarm how coarse and stiff the toilet-paper was. He suffered from haemorrhoids and had to use soft tissue.

'Tamura, did you bring some tissue paper?'

'I did. Why?' He looked over suspiciously from the bed where he sat, pulling from his bags the bottles of antacid and cold medication he had brought from Japan.

'Take a look in the toilet. I don't know of any country these days that uses such toilet-paper.'

The city reminded Imamiya of Changchun in Manchuria. As a soldier during the war he had been in Changchun briefly. Like Warsaw, in Changchun even the pavements in the bustling downtown region were smudged with mud and snow, and he remembered that all the Japanese walking along the streets had their faces and ears covered to ward off the cold.

'You're right.' Tamura had poked his head in the bathroom and returned with a sullen face. 'This is awful.' But since he was the one who had encouraged his friends to come to Warsaw, he had to mutter as if to himself: 'But, after all, this will give us something to talk about when we get home.'

After they had checked out the rooms, the men assembled once again in the vacant lobby, and at Shimizu's suggestion they went to the restaurant on the same floor. But it seemed less like a hotel restaurant than a wretched dance-hall, where two or three groups of foreign guests hunched over their plates and ate insipid food with knives and forks. In the corner a tiny band played a perfunctory waltz. Not one person applauded when they finished a number. As the men blithely slurped away at the soup they ordered, grumbling all the while about the miserable rooms in the hotel, Shimizu flipped through the pages of his itinerary.

'Tomorrow at 10 a.m. the city tour bus will pick you up at the hotel,' he announced.

'You expect us just to go to sleep like this tonight?'

'Women, is it? If it's women you want, you can pick them up in the snack-bar here in the hotel, but you can't take them to your rooms. The police are an awful nuisance, so be careful. The women will take you to their own apartments.' Shimizu spewed the words out in a monotone voice, as though he were reciting a memorized speech. He had been working part-time for the tour company for a year, but he had to provide the same information to the few groups of Japanese tourists who came to Poland. Again today he had to give the identical explanation in identical words. He knew that this was the only time they would listen to him carefully, staring into his face like obedient schoolchildren.

'But how do we get back here? Can we find taxis?'

'There are some taxis, but if you ask the woman she'll call one for you. Some women will even bring you here in their own cars.'

'Well, how considerate!' Tamura proudly looked around at the others. 'I told you how good Warsaw was!'

Once the subject of women came up, some life finally infused the stagnant air. After dinner, in high spirits they closed ranks and waddled in single file like ducks towards the snack-bar on the same floor of the hotel. When the invading force of Japanese entered the crowded snack-bar, the Poles who had been enjoying a light meal abruptly broke off their conversations.

'Mr Shimizu. Which women are we talking about?'

'They're scattered everywhere. Generally if a woman is having a beer by herself, she's one of them. They'll signal you with their eyes, so you'll know. Then I'll do the negotiating.'

Shimizu recalled that he had said exactly the same thing in precisely the same spot just three months earlier to a Japanese professor from a state university. Shimizu had seen the name of this professor, who had come to attend an international conference held in Warsaw, in Japanese newspapers and magazines. After the conference he went out of his way to exchange hugs and name-cards with the Polish scholars who had shared the podium with him, while meanwhile he was sending Shimizu, whom he treated like a research assistant, on all sorts of

errands. The evening before his departure, he surprised Shimizu by inviting him to the snack-bar and having a few drinks
with him. But when he suddenly smiled thinly and asked
Shimizu to find him a woman for the night, Shimizu felt
nothing but contempt for the man.

Over the year he had been guiding Japanese tourists for the
travel company, Shimizu had gradually determined that he
would turn himself into a sort of machine. A machine that
would welcome them at the airport, and see them off at the
airport. A machine that would check them into the hotel, and
get their room allocations for them. A machine that would
translate for shopping and sightseeing. A machine that would
take them to taverns and snack-bars where they could meet
women. A machine that would listen as they ridiculed the
poverty of Poland. A machine that would never let its own
thoughts or feelings show on its face. Had he not become such a
machine, he could never have done this pimp-like work for
Japanese tourists. When their stay was ended and he delivered
them to the airport, once he had bowed his head and wished
them a safe trip at the gate, he never had to deal with them
again for his entire life. Not one tourist had ever sent him a
single letter or even a postcard to thank him for his assistance.
They had merely used Shimizu as a convenient tool during their
brief stay overseas.

Half an hour later eight of the men had found companions for
the night. Shimizu asked the two remaining men if they wanted
to go to a bar in town to look for a woman. They looked at one
another and said they would give it up for tonight. Shimizu felt
relieved. Imamiya was one of the leftovers.

When the other eight Japanese had headed off for various
hotels with their women, Imamiya walked through the empty
lobby and went back to the room he shared with Tamura,
where he ran some bath-water. He wondered if the water,
which was brown when it first came out of the tap, would
eventually clear up. But though there seemed to be less rust the
more water he ran, it never did clear entirely. Stoically he
climbed into the tub, and after bathing he rinsed out his under-

pants. He had few regrets that he had not been able to frolic with a woman that night. Only two days before he came to Warsaw, a prostitute at the place de la Concorde in Paris had called to him from her car. Her dog sat in the passenger seat as she drove him to a cheap hotel next to the opera-house. Unlike his youthful days, he had reached an age when he no longer wanted a woman every night. And he had realized after several experiences that foreign women were not as he had imagined them while he was in Japan. The skin of their bellies and thighs was rough and scratchy as bark, and sometimes, thanks to the dark illumination in the assignation-rooms, their faces looked like demons. The moment the woman he had picked up in the Concorde stepped into the room she headed for the bathroom, where the sound of her urinating thoroughly revolted Imamiya as he sat listening through the door.

He put on his dressing-gown and took out a fountain-pen to write on the remaining postcards he had bought in France. He wrote to his daughter and her husband in Nagasaki that he had found the distinctive eau-de-Cologne and perfume they had requested. In his youth Imamiya had lived in Nagasaki, and his daughter had married into a family that had been close to his parents there. So, although he had lived in Osaka now for forty years, when he was drunk or perplexed the words that tumbled from his mouth were sometimes in the Nagasaki dialect.

He finished writing his postcards and lay down on the bed. The mattress was as hard as a steel plate.

The next morning, as the Japanese were climbing on to the sightseeing coach that had come to pick them up, a single platoon of soldiers had begun to form ranks on the Saski Plaza in front of the hotel. When Shimizu explained that every Sunday a military parade was held at the Tomb of the Unknown Soldier on this plaza, four or five of the Japanese quickly slung cameras over their necks and went racing out to the plaza still buried in snow. While the remaining Japanese watched from the bus with eyes hollow from lack of sleep, to the blare of a trumpet the soldiers raised their rifles with fixed bayonets to their shoulders and began to march, kicking away the snow. For a time snow continued to fall on the parade, then finally it stopped.

Half an hour behind schedule, the coach set out towards the Wisła River that runs through the city. Beside the driver's seat Shimizu tested his microphone and then began his exposition on the sights.

'The city of Warsaw that you are about to see may still seem to have much of the flavour of a city of old about it. You may think, when you see the medieval-style houses, the stone-paved plazas and the baroque buildings, that each has survived from former times, but in fact they were all constructed after the war. The Nazis, who occupied Warsaw in 1939, utterly destroyed the city at Hitler's command. Hitler ordered his underlings to remove the city and even the name of Warsaw from the map of the world for all eternity. The destruction was so complete that it was thought impossible that the city, which had been reduced to a mountain of bricks, could be rebuilt in even a hundred years. But after the war the people of Warsaw, relying on old sketches of the city, one by one carried stones, piled up bricks, and restored Warsaw just as it had been, from the colour of the walls to the shapes of the doors.'

Shimizu had repeated this speech many times over to Japanese tourists. He recited the canned commentary again today, and waited for the gasps of amazement. Before long, those exclamations echoed through the coach. The way in which the Japanese hurriedly turned their cameras to the window was always the same. Shutters clicked here and there.

'We are now driving through Zamkowy Plaza, also known as the Royal Castle Square. The bronze statue of Sigismund III, which stands in the middle of the square, and the Gothic Cathedral of St John have been reconstructed as they were before they were destroyed by German troops. The wounds of war still cut deep here in Poland, and the Polish people have not yet forgotten the scars inflicted on them by the German and Soviet armies. As you know, Poland is unquestionably a communist country, but a unique feature of this country is that ninety per cent of the population are simultaneously members of the Catholic Church. Communism and Christianity coexist in this land.'

This time nobody was listening. All he could hear was the shutter of a camera clicking on the right side of the coach. Oblivious to the interests of the Japanese tourists, Shimizu like a tape-recorder continued his commentary in a prosaic voice. He knew full well that not one of these Japanese sightseers had any interest in or curiosity about the commingling of communism and Christianity. It was part of Shimizu's subtle revenge on the Japanese tourists that he purposely droned on and on about the Polish Communist Party and the Church while knowing full well they were uninterested. It was his intangible retribution against fellow-countrymen who made him procure women for them along with everything else.

'I'm so sleepy.' Seated beside Imamiya, Tamura peered out of the bus window with puffy eyes. 'It was almost dawn when I came back to the hotel, you know. How was it? It was quite good. The women here have feeling. It's not just a business for them, they're providing a service for you.'

Before long Tamura's head collapsed clumsily against the window as he fell asleep. He was not alone; three or four other men had dropped off in their seats.

'To your right is Warsaw University. In former days this was the palace of the King of Poland.' Shimizu continued to talk into the microphone as if he were unaware of the dozing passengers. 'On the university campus the house where Chopin once lived is being used for classrooms.'

The spots where the Japanese took pictures were always predictable. The statue of the mermaid that stood on the banks of the Wisła River. The remains of the Jewish ghetto in the Muranów district. The bronze statue of Copernicus. Although many of them were sound asleep on the coach, once he mentioned these spots that appeared on postcards, they made the coach stop and charged out, scrambling to be the first to point their cameras in the appropriate direction. Once they had made the rounds of the famous tourist sites, they would return to the

Miasto market in the old part of the city, where they would have lunch. Then Shimizu would assist them in their shopping, after which they had free time until the evening.

When they reached the old city market some two hours later, Shimizu advised the group: 'We have just arrived at Miasto Plaza, the most beautiful square in all of Warsaw. There are many souvenir shops here, so feel free to buy whatever you wish. Please have lunch on your own here.'

As soon as the Japanese got off the coach, however, they flocked together and walked round the square. Several other tour coaches had parked on the stone pavement where frosty snow lingered like tiny sand-bars after the ebb tide, and tourists were peering into the surrounding souvenir shops. Nearly all the shops sold folk crafts, dolls dressed in native costumes and hand-woven fabrics. In disappointment someone remarked: 'These are all just childish trinkets. Isn't there any better stuff, Mr Shimizu?'

'Would you like to go to an antique shop? But the government won't allow the really good items to be taken out of the country.'

Like a group of scouts following their leader, the men refused to leave Shimizu's side. When one bought a doll, another bought a doll; when one took a look at some fabric, someone else examined fabric.

While the young female clerk was wrapping the doll Tamura bought, she smiled and began saying something to him. Since Tamura could understand no Polish, he turned to Shimizu and asked: 'What's she saying?'

'She's asking, since you're Japanese, you must know Father Kolbe.'

'Who's he?'

'He's the Christian Father most revered by the Polish people.'

'I don't know any of those "Amen" fellows.'

When Tamura waved his hand to answer 'No, no', the clerk nodded, but she looked rather saddened.

At the same shop Imamiya bought his youngest daughter, who was attending the university, a tapestry depicting a Polish farm woman. In London and Paris as well he had diligently cast about for souvenirs for his family, and had purchased a watch and a handbag for his wife. Every time he went back to his hotel room and placed a souvenir in his suitcase, Imamiya thought of himself as a good family man.

Although there was no reason why the men could not have had lunch or taken a walk separately, not one of them engaged in any activity apart from the rest, so they all ordered lunch at the same restaurant. The shop was famous for its shellfish and its excellent Polish meat dish known as *bigos*, and the Johnny Walker turned up the volume of the Japanese men's already boisterous voices. Tamura, his face a bright red, raised his glass of Johnny Walker to toast the Polish man quietly eating in the next seat. The middle-aged Pole, who looked like an office worker, smiled back and said: 'You're from the country where Father Kolbe worked, aren't you?'

'Again!' Exasperated, Tamura asked Shimizu: 'Kolbe. Just who is this Kolbe fellow?'

Without expression, Shimizu answered: 'Let's have him tell you.'

During his two years in Poland, Shimizu himself had heard the story of Father Kolbe over and over again from various people. But instead of telling the story himself, he deliberately asked the Polish man in the neighbouring seat, because he didn't want to offer any more than the essential service to his countrymen, and because he wanted to continue to function as a machine. The middle-aged Pole, dressed in an old, threadbare suit, continued to clutch his knife and fork as he nodded at Shimizu's questions.

'In 1941 Father Kolbe was confined in the Auschwitz internment camp for harbouring anti-Nazi sentiments. I think you all must have heard about this camp, where mass slaughters were carried out by means of forced labour and gas. The priest was suffering from tuberculosis, but he kept that to himself, and for three months he and the other captives were forced to dispose of the corpses from the gas chamber in that infernal prison.' Each time the Pole paused in his explanation Shimizu closed his eyes and translated in a lifeless voice. 'Three months later a prisoner escaped from the camp. The commandant placed the responsibility for the escape on all the prisoners, and as a warning he chose ten of them and put them in the hunger bunker.'

'What's a "hunger bunker"?'

Without any expression on his face, Shimizu relayed the question to the Polish man.

'A hunger bunker? It's a room where the people were kept in isolation, without bread or even a drop of water, until they died. There was another tiny execution chamber at Auschwitz, called the suffocation bunker. Many people were put in there, and the door was not opened until they had run out of oxygen and died.' The Pole's mouth twisted. 'On the day the prisoner escaped, the commandant made all the prisoners stand outside through the night, and then he chose the ten who were to be punished. One of them was a man named Gajowniczek. When his name was called, Gajowniczek began to weep at the thought of his wife and children. Just then a man stepped forward. It was Father Kolbe. He stood before the commandant and asked to be placed in the hunger bunker in place of Gajowniczek. Unlike this man, he said, I am a priest, and I have no wife or children. The commandant granted his request, and he was thrown into the subterranean chamber along with the other nine. Granted not even a cup of water, over a period of two weeks the captives began to die of starvation one after another, until only the priest and four other men remained alive. They were killed by a Nazi doctor who injected them with carbolic acid.'

It was silent inside the well-heated restaurant, and for a time the Japanese said nothing. Finally one of them muttered forlornly: 'What a horrid story!'

Suddenly the Pole remarked: 'Please go to Auschwitz while you're here.' Shimizu relayed this comment to the Japanese with the same blank look, but Tamura spoke for all when he shook his head and said: 'We're not going. Warsaw has been more than enough.' The Pole did not respond, but peered at the Japanese with dejected eyes.

'Dziękuję.' Shimizu thanked the man. 'Shall we head back to the coach?'

Relieved, the Japanese noisily rose from their chairs. With a cigarette dangling from his lips, Tamura called out from behind Shimizu: 'What's this Kolbe fellow got to do with Japan?'

'He spent two years as a missionary in Nagasaki.'

'What? Really? When was that?'

'I understand it was around 1930 or 1931.'

That afternoon there were still several tour coaches parked in the square, but perhaps because it was lunch-time they were deserted. Thanks to the sun seeping between the clouds, the muddy, icy snow began to melt. Walking alongside the others and carrying his sack of souvenirs, Imamiya thought back on the several foreign missionaries he had met in the streets of Nagasaki as he commuted to elementary school around 1930. At the time, the Imamiya house had stood on the slope leading to Ōura, and his father had operated a transport business. There in Ōura, which had been a foreign residential district since the early days of the Meiji period, it was not at all unusual to see foreigners climbing and descending the stone-paved hill. A number of foreign missionaries lived at the Ōura Catholic church and, dressed in their frocks, companies of them would often pass in front of the Imamiya house. Rumour had it that they had converted an abandoned Western-style house near the cathedral into a printing plant, where they published Bibles and prayer-books.

Whenever Imamiya ran into those missionaries on the hill, he, like the other children, would run and hide. He was frightened and apprehensive of the foreign missionaries who sported chin whiskers and wore long, peculiar black robes.

Kudō, a printer who came calling at his father's shop one day, remarked: 'Those men eat wretched food.' He had worked for about three months at the missionaries' printing office. 'They have so little. All they eat is cold rice and broth. And they sleep on a wooden plank with just a blanket over them.'

One day Imamiya rode in the passenger seat of his father's tiny delivery truck and visited the printing plant. Father and an apprentice were delivering a shipment of paper from the paper wholesaler at Sakura-chō. While his father and the apprentice did their work, Imamiya kicked around pebbles at the entrance to the Western-style house, which had become like a haunted house through exposure to the winds and rain. From time to time he heard the blast of steam whistles from the harbour. Just then, Imamiya noticed a single priest climbing from the bottom of the hill, using an umbrella in place of a walking-stick. The missionary, his head closely cropped, looked exhausted. He was frighteningly skinny. He seemed to be at pains to climb the hill, and half-way up he stopped, removed his sweat-clouded glasses and wiped them with a handkerchief while he got his breath back. Then he put his glasses on again and continued up the hill.

When the missionary saw Imamiya, an almost tearful smile ignited behind his round glasses, and in a faint voice he said: 'Konichiwa'. When Imamiya retreated two or three steps and hid behind the truck, the missionary disappeared in the direction of the printing shop.

For a long while Imamiya remembered the weary figure of that missionary, the sad smile that had flashed from behind his round glasses, and the hollow-cheeked face. He remembered the image, but he had no other impressions and virtually no other recollections of the foreigners. Thereafter the printing shop vanished and the foreign missionaries moved from Ōura to Sotomachi in the heart of the city.

The tour coach, loaded with the Japanese who had finished their lunch and shopping, set out once again. When they returned to the hotel near Saski Park, their time was free until dinner, but most of them, weary perhaps from their lack of sleep the previous night, kept to themselves in their rooms.

Following Tamura's lead, Imamiya lay down on his hard bed and tossed around until evening. Watching the snoring Tamura, who had wrapped a camel-coloured stomach-warmer round his abdomen, Imamiya thought of the name Kolbe, and wondered if by chance one of the missionaries he had encountered in the past had been Kolbe. A pain like a pinprick jabbed at the core of his heart. The figure of the languorous priest, with his round glasses and his smile, loomed before him, and the expression on the man's face stung Imamiya's heart. He got out of bed and shook his head to exorcize that expression. Tamura was still sleeping soundly. When Imamiya pressed his face against the window, the lights in Saski Park shone a pale white, and he could see hunched-over men wearing fur hats returning home from work through the lingering snow.

That night, Imamiya bought a woman.

After dinner, Shimizu escorted his Japanese clients to a night-club in Defilad Plaza. The show had already got under way, and an orange light in the middle of the crowded hall illuminated the tricks being performed by the entertainers.

Once they were seated, the Japanese men followed Shimizu's instructions and turned to look behind them, and their eyes all darted across the women who leaned against the back wall smoking cigarettes. Pretending to watch the show, the women were catching the eyes of the patrons. Imamiya's eyes met those of a woman who must have been about the same age as his eldest daughter, but she walked off towards the foreigners' seats. When he headed for the rest-room, he passed by the small, chestnut-haired woman. After he had washed his hands and came out again, she was standing in the same spot, staring up at him. Their transaction was concluded then and there.

'Did you find any good women?' Tamura brought his lips to Imamiya's ear. 'I got one who speaks Japanese. When I spoke to her, she winked and started saying: "Kombanwa, konichiwa, Mitsubishi, Sony." It's that woman over there. You can have her if you want.'

Imamiya answered that he had already found a partner, and half-way through the show he got up. Shimizu beckoned to him, handed him a piece of paper with the name of their hotel written on it, and told him to show it to the taxi-driver when he wanted to return.

The small woman was waiting for him at the exit of the night-club. She wore an overcoat with white fur round the collar, a fur hat and boots. When she saw Imamiya she smiled and went to fetch his coat from the cloakroom. Then she slipped her arm through Imamiya's and held on to him so that he would not slip on the icy snow outside the door. She began speaking to him in English, but since Imamiya could not understand her, he answered 'Hai, hai' in Japanese. She opened the door of a tiny car and had him get into the passenger seat. She started up the engine, but the car showed no signs of moving. When it finally surged forward, Imamiya said 'Ok', and she smiled and responded, 'Ok!'

They drove endlessly along the road, which was almost void of cars or people. Unlike Tokyo, on a winter's night the roads of Warsaw were deserted. Cold and shivering like an indigent, Imamiya felt the need to urinate again. From time to time the woman would speak to him in English, but he merely answered 'Hai, hai'.

Her apartment was in a five-storey building. They avoided the lift and climbed up the stairs that still smelled of cement. Their loud footsteps echoed in the empty apartment building. The woman opened the door and switched on the light. A refrigerator peered whitely from the eight-mat room, and he saw two chairs and a poster of some male actor hanging on the wall. When he came out of her bathroom, she had made him a whisky on the rocks. The bed was concealed behind a thick curtain. While he took a couple of gulps of his drink, she went to run some hot water in the bathroom. Imamiya stood up and went to the window to look outside, but all he could see was a building that appeared to be a warehouse.

Two or three books written in Polish stood on a tiny desk, and several photographs and religious pictures had been pasted on the wall directly behind the desk. One of the photos seemed to be of her family, and depicted a working-class husband and wife and a young girl. To the side was a picture of the Madonna, and mixed in with several Christmas cards was a reproduction of a portrait of a man drawn in black ink. The man was looking directly out at Imamiya, with a closely shaved head, round glasses and sunken cheeks. Imamiya remembered that weary expression. It was the foreigner who had painfully climbed the hill at Ōura that day in summer. It was the missionary who had stopped midway up the hill to wipe his clouded glasses, and had greeted Imamiya with a 'Konichiwa'.

When the woman came out of the bathroom in a dressing-gown, she spoke to Imamiya, who was staring intently at the portrait.

'That's Kolbe.'

Life

As we rode the special express train from Nagoya to Kanazawa, my travelling companion, the literary critic Yamamoto Kenkichi, abruptly asked me: 'Have you seen the film *The 203-Metre Hill*?' I had arranged to give a talk that evening at a meeting-hall in Kanazawa along with this man, who was my senior in the literary world.

'No, I haven't.'

'It's a splendid film. The title-song by Sada Masashi is particularly good. It's a sort of requiem.'

Recently Yamamoto has taken up popular music and serves as a judge for a prize given to the best recordings. He's so involved in the whole thing that he's known as the Shōji Tarō[1] of the literary world. That's because he reminds people of Shōji Tarō when he stands frozen like a statue in a bar crooning tunes like 'The Boat Song'.

And now, with his eyes fixed on the rain pouring outside the train window, he softly sang Sada Masashi's title-song. I don't remember much of it, but it started out by asking 'Do the mountains die? Do the rivers die?' and went on to lament the fact that only human beings had to die meaninglessly in wars.

I never did have a chance to see the Tōei film, *The 203-Metre Hill* that Yamamoto so enthusiastically recommended. I

---

1. Shōji Tarō (1898–1972) was a popular Japanese singer. He first went to work in Manchuria in 1923, the year Shusaku Endo was born. For more about his experience, see the story 'A Woman Called Shizu' below.

checked to see if it was on in Kanazawa, and looked for it after I returned to Tokyo, but it had long since ended its run.

Though I never saw that film, I still recall scenes on the same hill from an old film called *Emperor Meiji and the Russo-Japanese War*.

The troops under General Nogi ferociously assaulted the 203-Metre Hill at Lüshun. Countless soldiers perished before the Japanese forces reached the encampment of the enemy, which had been surrounded with *tochka* pillboxes. Though many fell along the way, the waves of attack by the Japanese army never ceased.

In the film the Japanese soldiers were dressed in deep-blue uniforms that bore no resemblance to the army fatigues I remembered from the Second World War, and they had white gaiters wrapped round their legs. When I saw them sprawled in the trenches while clouds of dust and exploding shells swirled over them, for some reason I was reminded of one soldier I met in my childhood.

An encounter between a boy and a soldier – however it may sound, there was nothing dramatic about the whole thing.

Around the time of the Manchurian Incident, I was attending elementary school in Dalian, which was near the Lüshun of 203-Metre Hill fame. My father was employed by a bank in Dalian.

Just as the title of the famous story by Kiyooka Takayuki, 'The Acacias of Dalian', suggests, that city established by Russians was luxuriant with acacia trees. But whenever I remember the city, somehow it is not the acacias that come first to my mind. It is rather the cold of the winters, the smoke from the chimneys of houses as it rose into the cold grey sky, and the groaning of *mache* horse carriages as they scurried across the frozen roadways.

Winter comes much earlier to Dalian than to Japan. No sooner are the voices of November heard than every house has lit a fire in a stove or a *pechka*. Soon snow begins to fall. Then it turns to frozen snow, which collects in filthy piles at the bases of the walls and gates of the houses. Eventually the soot that was belched from the chimneys stained the frozen snow black.

All through the winter, I made my way to elementary school slipping and falling on that frozen snow. I was a scrawny, spindly child, poor at studies and clumsy at sports. One moment at school I would be kicking up a disturbance, and the next instant I would be slumped in depression, no doubt because around that time a decisive rift had opened between my parents, and I had to endure within myself the desolation of their disharmony.

My source of comfort in those times was a battered harmonica. I don't even remember who gave it to me. The metal on the outside edge was slightly bent. I always kept the spit-stained harmonica in the drawer of my desk. I was, naturally, wretched at playing it, so I seldom took it with me to school, but when I was lonely or felt all alone in the world, I would play 'The Red Shoes' or 'The Bird in the Cage' on my harmonica.

I hated to come home from school and see my mother sunk in exhaustion from her quarrels with Father, so I always took the long way home. I would come to a halt at street-corners and stare at the white puffs of breath exhaled by the Manchurian horses hitched to the *mache* carriages that waited for patrons, or roughly kick up chunks of frozen ice with my shoes, doing everything I could think of to delay my return home by even a minute. I was a boy of only ten, but for the first time that year I came to know, as well as a common child can, the bitterness of life.

On one such day when I got home a large motor cycle was parked in front of our gate. It belonged to the neighbourhood doctor, who always donned his riding-boots and rode his motor cycle to examine an ailing patient.

My first thought when I saw the motor cycle was that my mother might be ill. But she was not. The doctor, who also served as something like a neighbourhood association leader, was making the rounds of each house in the area to relay orders from the city government. 'Some soldiers are going to be staying with you,' he told me as I came upon him in the entryway trying to stuff his feet into his riding-boots. 'You'll enjoy that, won't you?'

Mother instead seemed upset by this sudden directive foisted upon her. Yet I was elated, not so much by the fact that soldiers would be staying in our house, but because the gloomy atmosphere would change if even for just one night because of their advent.

Since the previous year, it was no longer unusual in Dalian to have Japanese soldiers stay in people's homes rather than in barracks. These soldiers would stay in the homes of Japanese for one or two nights, and then be loaded on to trains and shipped to the battlefields deep in the Manchurian interior.

The next day at school, I proudly announced to my friends the news we had received. The families of some of my friends had received similar orders, but ours was the only household providing accommodation for four soldiers, which tickled my petty sense of pride. In any case, for the next several days I was able to forget a good deal of the pain and loneliness of returning to my bleak home.

On the day the ship bringing the soldiers from Japan was supposed to arrive in Dalian harbour, I listened with only half my brain to what went on in the classroom, and the moment school was finished, I raced home. I flung my knapsack on to the floor of the entryway and called out to our old housekeeper, but the soldiers had not yet arrived in the city.

Night came. The children from the neighbourhood came tumbling down the icy road, shouting in unison: 'They're here!' At their cries, even the adults came out of their houses, waiting for the echo of marching boots to draw gradually nearer.

A column of soldiers, led by a young officer, appeared in the street. Then, beneath the cold night air and the admiring gaze of the children, the young officer barked crisp orders, lining his men up and ordering a roll-call. He determined the distribution of his men in consultation with the motor-cycle doctor and representatives from the neighbourhood, then announced these assignments to the troops.

Night had already begun to fall, but here and there voices of families exchanging greetings with the soldiers could be heard, the beams of torches spiralled along the ground, dogs startled by the commotion howled, and the street took on the air of a festival eve. Father, who had returned from work, located the four soldiers who had been allocated to our house. I was on top of the world.

Once the soldiers came into our house, it was filled with the potent smells of leather belts and sweat. Mother and the housekeeper scurried around the kitchen, while the soldiers, emerging one after another from the bath, removed their jackets and sat down to drink *sake* with Father in the parlour, where a stove blazed redly. Time and again I caught a peek of them from behind the parlour door, then raced back into the kitchen.

'Young man. Come here.' Inside the parlour, an older soldier noticed me and beckoned to me with his hand. He put his arm round me, and I froze there between his legs, trying to endure the smell of alcohol on his breath.

'Well, young fellow, I don't expect you drink *sake*, do you? Would you like some bean jelly? Give him some bean jelly.' He ordered the young soldier who was sitting in the far corner of the room to share some of his bean jelly with me. This young soldier had a face as round and white as a doll's, and his cheeks were red. And though the other three soldiers were dressed in casual clothes after their baths, he alone still wore his uniform jacket, and he drank little *sake*.

They gave me a lot of bean jelly and candy. With intense interest they questioned my father about the cold climate in the interior of Manchuria.

'I hear it gets down to 20 or 30 degrees below zero. I don't think there's any place in Japan that gets so cold. Is it true that even the snot in your nose freezes right up?' the elder soldier inquired.

'It's true,' Father nodded.

Evidently they continued eating for some time. I say 'evidently' because it wasn't long before Father ordered me to bed. I crawled into the bedding the housekeeper had spread out on the floor for me, happy that an entire day had passed without any strife between my parents, and for a short while I played on my harmonica. Usually the voices of my father and mother arguing in the parlour would carry all the way to my bedroom at night. Not wanting to hear their fighting, I would always pull the heavy covers over my head, but tonight I didn't have to do that.

When I woke up the next morning, the soldiers were already gone. Apparently they had left very early on some kind of exercise.

They returned that evening, emitting smells of leather and sweat. From the entryway they called out greetings to my mother and disappeared into the parlour that served as their bedroom. From the hall the housekeeper called out: 'The bath is all ready.'

From one side of the entryway I heard sounds like a wet towel being snapped repeatedly against a wall. Each snap was followed by a low, strangled cry.

I peered out of the window. The pale young soldier who had given me the bean jelly and candy the night before was being made to stand at attention by the wall next to the entryway. Another soldier, standing in front of him, was saying something and slapping him across the face with an open hand. An echo like the cracking of a whip reverberated each time he was struck, and the pale soldier staggered, but he quickly recovered his posture and received the next blow.

My astonishment was so great I could not move from the window. This was the first time I had ever seen one adult strike another.

Someone called out from the behind me. 'Young man. Could you get me a glass of water?' I turned around, and the elder soldier, just out of the bath, stood there holding his towel. He seemed to be the highest ranking of the four soldiers, and the night before he had been the first to use the bath.

He noticed the sound coming through the window and walked over beside me to look outside. Then with a grin he said: 'I'll bet your teachers hit you like that when you cheat at school.'

Frightened, I retreated to my study. Smoke from a *pechka*

swirled from the chimney of the house beyond the wall, while the gnarled branches of the bare acacia trees jutted into the gloomy sky. I pulled my harmonica from the drawer and played on it for a while.

When Father returned from work that night, he again drank *sake* in the parlour with the soldiers. They seemed to have grown more familiar, because I repeatedly heard laughter louder than the previous night erupting from the room. But the scene I had witnessed earlier weighed on my mind, and I had no desire to peek in on them through the parlour door.

Still holding my harmonica, I went quietly to the entryway, trying not to let anyone in the parlour notice me. I wanted to go outside, but it was already cold. In the dark entrance, the shadowy figure of a man was crouched down doing something. It was the young soldier who had been pummelled, and he was polishing the boots of his comrades. Even a boy like me knew at once that it was his duty as a low-ranking soldier to tend to the needs of the others.

He glanced quickly at me and went on with his work. For my part, I leaned against the pillar at the entrance, my harmonica still crammed in my mouth, and quietly watched his hands move back and forth as he polished the boots. He didn't appear to have any inkling that I had seen him being slapped.

'Don't you drink *sake* . . .?' I asked in a faint voice.

He turned his eyes up at me and said: 'No, I don't.'

I blew softly on my harmonica. But he looked as though he didn't hear, so I began to play a clumsy rendition of 'The Red Shoes', making several mistakes along the way. I assumed he would say something like 'You're good, young man', but he said not a word.

'Where are you going when you leave Dalian?'

'The interior of Manchuria.'

'Where in Manchuria?'

'I do not know.'

He answered me as though he were speaking to one of his superior officers. It was as though he was afraid that the elder soldier or the comrade who had struck him would appear at any moment from the end of the dark corridor.

Neither of us said anything for a while.

Suddenly he asked: 'What year in school are you?'

'Third grade. . . .'

Again we were silent. I twisted the harmonica around in my hand, and then suddenly, holding it out to him, I said: 'I'll give you this.'

I had no idea why I said that. It was a battered harmonica, caked with spittle, but to me it was a treasure. Playing it had soothed my mind whenever I head my father and mother fighting. My impulsive attempt to give the harmonica to this soldier may have been motivated by a desire to comfort him as he crouched there all alone polishing those boots, or perhaps I had projected my own loneliness on to the figure of this man who had stood in the dark night and surrendered himself without complaint to a beating.

'I'll give you this.'

But he stayed hunched over and shook his head. 'I don't want it.'

My hand still held the harmonica out to him. As though I were trying to forge some faint, secret link between myself and him by giving him the harmonica.

'I don't want it.' He stared at me, responding as if in fear.

And that was the end of it. Early the next morning he and the other soldiers left our house, formed into ranks and, at an order from their commanding officer, disappeared from our street. After that the fighting in Manchuria escalated.

For many years, I had forgotten all about that soldier. But ten years ago, while I was watching the film *The Emperor Meiji and the Russo-Japanese War* in a cinema in the suburbs, when I saw waves of soldiers storming the 203-Metre Hill, falling one after another to enemy bullets, I suddenly thought of him. I thought of that soldier, who had been frightened of something, rejecting my attempt to form a fragile bond of the heart with him with the words 'I don't want it'.

About half a year later, the housekeeper who worked for us

decided to return to her home in Kyushu. The reason she gave was that her son and daughter-in-law had agreed to look after her, but when I consider it now, it seems to me that perhaps she too had come to dislike the dark cloud that hung over our home.

Her home town was a place called Hondo, on Amakusa Island in Kyushu. It was a source of great pride to her that her family owned a piece of land encircled with fields of *mikan* trees and with a beautiful view of the sea, and she often boasted to me about it. The more she bragged about it, the more I came to feel that she had idealized the home she had been forced to leave for some reason, and that the very act of idealization had become a kind of reason for living in her mind.

After she returned to Japan, a Manchurian houseboy came to assist us.

He was a pedlar who often came through the neighbourhood selling yellow pickled radishes. I suppose he must have been around seventeen or eighteen. When Mother proposed that he move in and help with our housework, he immediately agreed, arriving the very next day with a tiny bag of personal belongings.

He was scrawny, and always had a look of apprehension on his face. He may have been so skinny because his livelihood didn't provide him with enough to eat. The look of fear on his face perhaps came from the fact that he was Manchurian. Come to think of it, when most Manchurian people crossed paths with a Japanese policeman a look of subservience or of fear would dart across their faces, and that was just the kind of expression our houseboy always wore.

All the more because of his scrawny body and terror-stricken face, he was very kind to us. He was particularly attentive in looking after me, I who was much younger than he.

When the winter became severe, primary school students like me would arrive at school very early. A thick layer of ice covered the roads, which had been exposed to temperatures colder than 10 below zero all through the night, and sometimes as we walked along them we would flop down on our bottoms. The primary-school boys loved to come crashing down on their behinds, but a steep hill separated my house and the school, and walking down it was perilous.

Our houseboy always accompanied me to the base of that hill. I wore a thick overcoat, a scarf round my neck and a pair of gloves, but the only protection he wore against the elements was the tattered pair of high rubber boots that Father had given him. I still remember it well. Each morning he would descend the hill in front of me, so that his body could support mine in case I should slip. His clumsy Japanese, cautioning me over and over again to 'Taking care!' 'Taking care, young master. Taking care!'

He would walk ahead of me, creating a wall of protection as I made my way to school, even on days when the snow, carried on the frosty wind, lashed at me. Blizzard-like flakes of snow beat mercilessly against his face and body, but thanks to him I avoided having it pound directly on me.

Being as young as I was then, I thought this arrangement perfectly normal. It seemed like natural work for him, since he was older, and since he was our houseboy. I had no idea how difficult it had been for him to endure the pain of the cold wind striking his face and arms. My chest aches now as I think of him saying: 'Taking care, young master. Taking care!'

As winter drew to a close, the relationship between my mother and father took a decisive turn for the worse. The more their marriage disintegrated, the more I put on the mask at school, romping about in feigned good spirits, doing everything in my power to keep my teachers and friends from detecting the dark feelings in my heart. But once classes were over and I started home, with my empty alumite lunch box clattering around in my knapsack, I reverted to my true face. The frozen roads. Smoke rising into the dark sky from houses that had lit their *pechkas*. With melancholy in my eyes, I purposely made longer and longer detours on my way home. At the youth hall or at the Yamato Hotel, where I sometimes stopped to loiter, the rooms were warmed by steam heat. I would look on endlessly as the adults bustled in and out.

One day I returned home very late. I had intentionally delayed my return, even though I knew my worried mother would reprimand me harshly for coming back so late. I think I must have done it in a spirit of rebellion against my parents, who had come to ignore my very existence as the hostility between them had mounted. I had wanted to retaliate against my father and mother.

I climbed the hill to our house, listening as the lunch-box clanked in my knapsack. A deep-purple evening haze had mingled with the cold, and the road had already started to freeze over. A *mache* carriage that had started to climb the hill seemed to have abandoned the attempt, and diverted to another road. That was when I saw him standing coldly half-way up the hill. At Mother's orders, or, actually, because he himself had been worried about me, he had come looking for me, since I was so late.

Mother scolded me mercilessly. No matter how ruthlessly she rebuked me, I stubbornly turned away, refusing to apologize. She slapped me two or three times. He had been sitting in the corner, listening with concern, and now he hurried to her side and cried fervently: 'Madam, stopping! Madam, stopping!'

The beating only fortified my rebellious spirit. I began to hate parents who could not comprehend their own child's grief. And ultimately I took revenge on my mother by doing something even more extreme than coming home late from school. I stole a ring that my mother treasured and sold it. I knew where she kept the ring with its blue gem, and it was no trouble at all to remove it from her drawer.

After I stole the ring, I took it to a notions store run by a Manchurian man on the road to school. Inside the shop, lined with all manner of goods from tea-leaves to a smattering of Manchurian pharmaceuticals, two men held the ring up to the light bulb, twisting it around until finally they gave me a single silver coin worth 50 sen.

I bought some sweets with the coin, then agonized over where I might hide the change. Even in my child's mind, I was convinced that if I hid the money somewhere in the house, I should be subjected to a grilling if by some chance it were discovered. So after much deliberation, I buried the change in a corner of the school yard.

My landmark was three tall poplar trees that stood at the edge of the yard. Every autumn the poplars shed their yellow leaves over the ground. We would gather up the dried leaves, and two of us would grasp either end of the stems and pull; the boy whose stem was torn was the loser.

After school I made sure no one was watching, then I buried a portion of the change in the ground, and on my way home I spent the rest on food. The money was soon gone.

Some two weeks later, Mother discovered her ring was missing. It never occurred to her that I might be the thief. Her suspicions were directed towards our Manchurian houseboy.

'I'm sure it's that Manchurian. No matter how nicely we treat him, this is how he thanks us,' she told me.

I said nothing. I neither confessed what I had done, nor denied that he was guilty.

The next day, the doctor who served as neighbourhood association leader arrived on his motor cycle. I listened in as he chatted with Mother, 'You really ought to report him to the police, Ma'am. It does no good being kind to these Manchurians.'

'But. . . .' Mother was hesitant. 'There's no proof that he stole it.'

'That's why you must have the police make a thorough investigation. If they do, he'll fess up.'

As I listened to them talk, I realized for the first time that what I had done was so awful it was a matter for the police. Anxiety clutched so tightly at my chest I thought it might collapse. I felt I must say nothing, no matter what happened.

The doctor was in our house for almost two hours, after which he again mounted his motor cycle and left. The droning of the motor cycle as it drove into the distance rumbled endlessly in my aching chest.

Mother, of course, did not report the houseboy to the police. But when I returned from school the next day, he was nowhere to be seen. Even though I knew he was gone, I stood outside the tiny room next to the kitchen where he always slept and feebly called out his name two or three times. His terrified face fluttered ceaselessly before my eyes.

At my age now, I often wake up in the middle of the night. With my eyes open, I remember and ponder the lives of the people who have passed through my life, and sometimes I am gripped by feelings that are a jumble of embarrassment and regret, and I emit a faint cry like a moan. Each time I think of that Manchurian houseboy, a muffled sound like a moan escapes my lips. . . .

Last autumn, I boarded a large ship and returned to visit Dalian for the first time in forty-seven years. My heart swelled with emotion.

Though I had not seen the city in forty-seven years, the streets looked much the same. Not a single new building had been constructed, and the old hotels and parks and banks and schools were still being used as hotels and parks and banks and schools. Only the name of the city had changed; the streets and plazas and roadside trees were each as I remembered them. The buildings that had seemed so broad and tall to me now looked cramped and squat. Everything had grown old, been stained with soot and blackened. A friend who had accompanied me muttered: 'It's like a ghost town.'

The October sky was cold and the colour of lead. While continuing to humour our interpreter, who encouraged us to visit the factories and the people's communes, I had him take me to the school I had attended and the house I had lived in so many years ago.

The name of my school had been changed to Lüda City Number Nine Middle School, but the school gate, the buildings and the playgrounds were virtually unchanged from my memory of them. Some teachers took me into a room where a class was in session. It happened to be an English lesson being taught by a female teacher. Even after I came into the room, the students continued to stare at the blackboard, hardly casting a sidelong glance in my direction. Perhaps they had been trained not to avert their eyes even when someone was observing their class.

The female teacher read the English text with excellent pronunciation, and the students responded adroitly. Each student sat properly, and not one of them glanced out of the window or poked the student next to them as I had done in the old days. Every student looked bright, and their expressions contained none of the shadows of life's loneliness and sorrow such as had clouded my brow when I was their age. I couldn't say whether that was good or proper for them. I couldn't say, but I felt a little discontented about it.

They let me look at the chemistry room and a geography class, and then we went out on to the cold playground. My ears hurt a little from the cold. The teachers wore genial smiles on their faces, and over and over again they talked about the 'modernization of China'.

There was not a soul in the playground. It, too, was just as it had been. Just as in the past, across the way I could see the building that had been the headquarters of the Manchurian Railway, and from there the long wall continued, until at the point where it ended poplar trees soared into the sky. The poplars, as before, were tall, and there were still three of them. I had buried the money I obtained from selling Mother's ring at the foot of those poplars, then feigned total innocence. And I had passed the transgression on to our Manchurian houseboy, and continued to play the innocent. 'Taking care, young master. Taking care, young master!' Flakes of snow had stabbed mercilessly at his face, twisted from the cold. . . .

The teachers at the school naturally detected nothing in my expression. They saw us to the gate of the school, where they clapped their hands respectfully as we left.

A Sixty-year-old Man

Is it because I've become old? Lately I haven't slept very soundly, and in the course of one night I have several dreams, each of them independent of the others. As soon as one dream is over, I wake up. Once my eyes are open, I stare into the darkness, thinking only of my approaching death. I turned sixty this month.

Recently I had the following dream. I'm in a dark room. I'm face to face with Akutagawa Ryūnosuke. Akutagawa is wearing a grey, wrinkled, unlined kimono, and he stares down with folded arms. He does not say a single word, but suddenly he stands up, passes through the rattan blind behind him, and goes into the next room. I knew that the adjoining room was the world of the dead, but before long Akutagawa came back into the room. Then I woke up. After I opened my eyes, I wondered vaguely why I had started having such gloomy dreams with greater frequency. Beside me, my wife breathed peacefully in her sleep.

Of course I've never told my wife about any of these dreams. Even if I did relate them to her, they wouldn't arouse her interest. For a long while I have worn the mask of good husband and good father (though it seems odd to be saying this myself) inside my own home. But though I have donned the mask with my own hands, that doesn't mean I have forced myself to play some role that wasn't truly a part of me. There's something in my personality that instinctively adopts an attitude of gentleness towards others. But, naturally, the face of the good husband and father is not all there is to me, and I have another face that my family knows nothing about. I imagine the same thing could be said by any husband. . . .

Each and every morning at ten, I unlock the door to my office near Harajuku, and I step into the four-and-a-half mat room with closed curtains. When I sit down at my desk, which is littered with a confusion of papers and dictionaries and books, my face becomes all my own, a face unconstrained by others. I think that face must be a gloomy one, like the dreams I have every night. Sometimes as I look into the mirror, I think this face must be what in Buddhism is called the 'face of dark delusion'. A world where I search for salvation but have yet to discover the light; the downcast face of Akutagawa Ryūnosuke that I encountered in my dreams.

It's that face I wear when I start writing my fiction. 'Start writing', yes, but now that I'm sixty I seldom do any writing where I'm hounded by a deadline. What I'm working on now is a thorough rewrite of the *Life of Jesus*, which I first published over fifteen years ago, but I haven't decided which publisher to place it with.

I'm dissatisfied when I read the *Life of Jesus*, which I wrote more than fifteen years ago. I'm not saying it's shallow, but at the age of forty-five or so I still hadn't read the Bible very thoroughly. I hadn't chewed on each word of it with my own teeth, and many portions of my work rely a bit too heavily on interpretations by Western scholars.

For instance, in examining why Jesus was abandoned by those who had acclaimed Him just one day before – and not just abandoning Him, but treating Him sadistically, tormenting and beating Him, spitting on and finally killing Him – I didn't consider that any more than the result of simple mob psychology. It's quite clear that Jesus, who preached love, was murdered as a political criminal, but I didn't even attempt to ponder why they were all gripped with the desire to abuse Him.

As I reread the book I wrote more than fifteen years previously, such sources of dissatisfaction popped up one after another from this page, then that page. I might mention that the place where I composed my *Life of Jesus* so many years ago was this same small, musty office. (In this four-and-a-half mat room, I can't work unless I close the curtains even in broad daylight and sit at the desk. The appropriate level of darkness and the appropriate clamminess in the room provide me with the same feeling of liberation as that of being in my mother's womb.) At that time, I had optimistically thought that after a decade or so the doubts and questions which arose as I read the New Testament would be resolved, and that I could compliantly believe it all. But ten years later, even now fifteen years later at the age of sixty, I still have no feeling of resolute calm within, and sometimes the blue hell-fires of doubt flare up even more miserably than before.

This tiny room has hardly changed over the decade and a half. The desk and chair, the clock on top of the desk and the work-lamp and Chinese brush-holder are just as they were then. On the wall hang several old framed maps I bought when I was a student in Lyon in my twenties. My habit of hunching over the desk and writing with a number 3B pencil is the same now as it was then. But today I can't work without the bifocals that I never needed when I was forty-five. It's not just my eyes, either; my entire body itself has gradually been gnawed away at, eroded and enfeebled by old age. In former days it didn't bother me at all to sit in this chair for hours at a time, but now when I sit in the same position for two hours, an ache gently spreads from my waist down to my groin. I've been plagued with sciatica for the past three years.

To avert an attack of neuralgia, at a fixed time every afternoon I leave my office and go out for a walk, slipping a body-warmer into my hip pocket and throwing on a fairly thick coat. Yoyogi Park and the large grounds and plaza of the NHK broadcast network are not far from my office, and I can walk there without being bothered by cars.

But recently I haven't been to Yoyogi Park, where young mothers bring their children to romp, or to the NHK plaza, where young people play badminton. I go straight to the Omote Sandō district at Harajuku.

Actually, in one of the back streets at Omote Sandō there's a coffee shop called Swan, and since this past winter it's become my habit to sit near the window at Swan for about an hour, beginning at three in the afternoon. I know that if I sit by the window, at some time after three, young high-school girls on their way home from school will stop by the cake shop opposite to buy ice-cream. Watching them, I've learned that when they're in a group, they frolic and play around together, but when they walk by themselves in this road, they are conscious of the gaze of others to an almost ridiculous degree. I find that amusing.

Sometimes, three or four rowdy-looking girls come into the coffee shop. I can tell they're trying to brazen it out because they march into the coffee shop, which is off-limits to students, still dressed in their school uniforms. Even an old man like me can tell the kind of game they're playing from the way they talk and the deliberately long skirts they wear. When they toss a contemptuous look at their classmates and defiantly throw open the door of the coffee shop and walk past me, my nose picks up the same sort of pristine smell you encounter in a grove of trees in early spring. At first I thought it was the smell of their uniforms, but eventually I realized that it was actually the odour of the bodies of girls this age.

They jabbered on without interruption. All manner of peculiar words that I couldn't understand peppered their conversation. I finally worked out that in their group boys were called 'dudes', E.T. was the name they gave to their menstrual periods, and that homework was 'the bore'. They talked like boys, rudely, and sometimes they left out verbs altogether, apparently getting their meanings across to one another just by lining up words. Their faces, forbidden as they were from wearing make-up, were covered with pimples, and their cheeks were red as though engorged with blood. But in their faces and throats I sensed the throb of life that pervades a grove in early spring, a throb that is gone by the time a young woman reaches twenty-two or twenty-three, and sometimes I would instinctively shut my eyes in amazement.

Nearly twenty years ago I had a conversation with an old man. He was a scholar of woodblock prints, and he confided to me that, after he finished his lectures at the university, he would go home and don a wig, slip into a pair of jeans, put on some black sun-glasses, and set out dressed as a young man to go-go dance. 'Why would you do something like that?' I asked him, and with an embarrassed grin he answered: 'It's a dark basement dance-hall, and everybody's caught up in their dancing, and nobody thinks I'm an old man. Even young women under twenty dance with me. When those young ladies dance, they start sweating a little around their throats. They give off the faint aroma of sweat. That smell of sweat has an eroticism to it that you don't find in older women. I can close my eyes like this and inhale that smell to my heart's content.'

I was still forty or so when I had that conversation with the elderly professor, and I couldn't understand in any tangible sort of way the sorrow and loneliness of growing old. But now that I'm as old as he was then, I understand. How it feels to close your eyes and inhale the aroma of sweat exuded by a woman not yet twenty. How it feels for someone who will soon bid farewell to this world to make the desperate effort to suck in the smells of life at its zenith. . . . Sitting in my window seat, recalling that conversation, I stole glances at the high-school girls.

How aware were they of my gaze? I think, in fact, that the little imps knew instinctively just what I was up to. They must have realized it and yet they continued their conversations with a deliberate look of nonchalance on their faces.

One day, while I was half listening to their conversations, one of them remarked: 'Well, I think he likes you, Nami.'

'How would I know?' her friend answered.

'What if you sent him some chocolates on Valentine's Day? Then you could see how he'd react.'

The girl named Nami had slits for eyes. She grinned in a sweet, idiotic sort of way. But her face was as artless as that of a middle-school girl's. She stood up without answering and headed for the rest-room at the back of the shop.

'Hey, hey, aren't we Little Miss Important!' her friends taunted her from behind. 'Don't we know how to play innocent! It's because you act like that that Mr Matsuda's always taken in.' Half-way to the rest-room, Nami turned back and grinned sweetly, then from behind the door she leaned out and shook her fist at her friends. It was an utterly meaningless conversation and a meaningless gesture to these girls, but an indescribable sensation raced through my heart in that moment.

Why did I feel that sensation? I couldn't explain it then. But as I walked down the wide slope running beside Yoyogi Park on my way back to my office from Harajuku, I felt as though I had witnessed the same scene somewhere in the distant past. And I was certain that I had felt the same sensation then. But I couldn't say just when that had happened. Experiencing that same sort of beguiling feeling you have when you find yourself standing before a scene you have witnessed in your dreams, I opened the door to my office. When I sat down in front of the desk, I thought of Stavrogin's confession in Dostoevsky's novel. That's it – the young woman's gesture was just like the scene in *The Possessed* when Stavrogin assaults the twelve-year-old girl, Matryosha.

One summer evening, knowing her parents are away, Stavrogin visits the young Matryosha's home. And he rapes her. When it is all over, she opens her large eyes and looks him hard in the face, and then suddenly she turns up her nose and shakes her tiny fist at him in a menacing gesture. Then she leaves the room, preparing to hang herself in the little chicken-coop-like shed next to the bathroom. Though he realizes what she is going to do there, Stavrogin makes no move to stop her, but instead stares fixedly at a tiny red spider that is crawling on a geranium leaf by the window.

Four years after that incident, while travelling in Germany, Stavrogin dreams of a painting by Claude Lorrain. It was a work he painted as he visualized an earthly paradise. 'Beautiful men and women had lived here. They lived each day happy and innocent,' writes Dostoevsky. 'The forests echoed with their joyful songs. . . . The sun shed its bright rays on the islands and the sea, beaming down upon its children. It was a remarkable dream . . . the most unlikely illusion that has ever been seen, but for which mankind has offered up all its powers throughout its whole existence, for which it has sacrificed everything, for which it has died on the cross and for which all its prophets have been murdered.' But in that moment, within that shimmering light, that paradisaical glimmer, Stavrogin sees a vision of Matryosha, shaking her head at him and brandishing her tiny fist, her eyes flashing as though feverish. The vision shocks him profoundly.

The first time I read this passage, yes, it was forty years ago, when I was still a student. In my dormitory room by the Shinanomachi station, where I ceaselessly listened to the sounds of the National Railway trains coming and going, I felt an inexpressible distaste for Stavrogin. His act of defiling an unknowing, innocent young girl both filled me with disgust and pricked my curiosity. And just now, the 'rest-room' and 'the young woman shaking her fist' had brought that scene back to me.

After that, whenever I went to Swan and sat down by the window and picked that young woman out of the group of high-school girls, I always thought of that scene. A sixty-year-old man steals glances at a young woman of no more than sixteen or seventeen. The story told me by the aged professor I now applied to myself. The only one of the girls to attract my curiosity was the one who spoke so sloppily, the one who grinned broadly like an idiot, the one on whose face flickered an expression that reminded me the most of the young Matryosha.

Once a week my ageing wife comes to clean my office. On that day I don a different face from the one I wear when I am here alone. No, that's not quite the right way to put it. It would be more accurate to say that I go back to being who I am at home. Because there is no exertion, no play-acting, no hypocrisy involved.

After lunching together, we go out for a walk. But I've never taken my wife to Swan, or told her about the high-school girls. They have nothing to do with the thirty years that she and I have lived together. It's been a warm winter this year, and as we walk along dodging the cars that speed past, the warm sun beating on our shoulders feels good.

We sit down on a bench in one corner of the NHK plaza and watch some young people playing badminton in the distance. My wife peers at them. I have the feeling I know what's going through her mind at such times. A long time ago – yes, a very long time ago, we had been that young, and we had gone to the same university. Over the past thirty five years I've endured a long illness, we've travelled overseas together, at times we've comforted one another, or wounded each other with our mutual egotism: in short, we've experienced most of what all married couples go through. And now, our backs towards the gentle sun that weighs almost heavily on our eyelids, we sit side by side on a bench like two little birds. When I was studying abroad, the elderly French couple who had been my landlords had once said, 'We know each other so completely we don't have to say a word', and I suddenly remembered that remark. Now that I've reached sixty, however, I've at last come to realize that they were wrong. Not even married couples know each other completely. But if I were to say that, all my wife would do is give me a pained look. There is no reason at this point in our lives to cause pain to this woman, whose hair is speckled with threads of silver, so unlike her youthful days.

After she leaves, the office becomes all mine again. Steam rises quietly from the electric heater. I rewrite the scene of the crucifixion in my *Life of Jesus*. I struggle to remember the old town in Jerusalem, which I visited three or four times with my wife in an attempt to draw near to that scene. The city has changed since Jesus' day, but some of the atmosphere of those times still lingers in the old town. The pathways littered with donkey dung and urine; the streets penned in by grimy walls, twisting and turning and becoming blind alleys. On the walls of various buildings hung copper plaques that read: 'Here Jesus collapsed as He carried the cross', 'Here stood the palace of Herod, who passed judgement on Jesus.' Each time we came across one of those, my wife bowed her head and offered a prayer, and I followed her example. I prayed earnestly, with no guile. The other me prayed from the depths of his heart.

I could hear the tumult of the masses as they mocked Jesus, stoned Him and spat upon Him. That's how a mob behaves. (I had seen more than my fill of such mobs during the war, and again after the war.) These were the same people who had run fervently after Jesus just the day before. Why had they changed so completely? Fifteen years ago, I had written in my own book: 'It was because they realized that Jesus was an impotent man who could not bring any of their dreams to reality. It was because they realized that this man could do nothing to fulfil their dream of driving the Romans from their nation.' That interpretation is not incorrect. But it is a conclusion reached by several scholars, not a statement that I had ground with the teeth of my own experience. Something was missing.

My house is located about an hour by train from Tokyo, so the temperature in winter is 2 or 3 degrees lower. As a result, some nights I suffer a bit because of my sciatica. And it's not just the neuralgia. Until I reached fifty-five, I had some measure of confidence in my physical body, but then, maybe because of the operation I had on my nose, my body changed dramatically. Old age suddenly began to flaunt its ugly face in various parts of my body. It started with laboured breathing and dizziness, then my appendages began to get cold, and one after another my teeth went rotten.

A poster featuring Uehara Ken and Takamine Mieko hanging on the platform at Harajuku Station reads: *Those Beautiful Years of Maturity*. It's fine to call old age the 'years of maturity', but that doesn't change its essence. There is no fundamental way to grow old beautifully. It's obvious to me just from looking at my body and my face in the mirror that old age is brutally ugly. Drab, lifeless hair, blotched skin – and it isn't just the face and body that grow ugly. Ugliness also means that tranquility and peace of mind have yet to visit your heart even when you're past sixty. Even at sixty God won't grant me such feelings, and when I open my eyes in the darkness separating dream from dream, suddenly the fear of death stabs at me acutely. The extinction of my own body. Never again being able to see the light of morning, the shapes of the streets, the movements of people. Never smelling the aroma of warm coffee. . . . At such thoughts, my chest aches as though gouged with a sharp knife. Where will I breathe my last? When will it happen? I try not to think about it. I try to fall asleep quickly in order to escape such thoughts. The ugliness of old age is the inability to be free of such wretched attachments to life.

On Sundays, one corner of Yoyogi Park and the road that runs alongside it are packed with onlookers who have come to watch the young members of the 'bamboo-shoot' generation. The spectators watch enthusiastically as the young men and women form circles here and there and begin a peculiar dance to music from cassette-players. I'm one of the observers. The bamboo-shoot teenagers sport long, Korean-style robes of white or pink, and both male and female participants wear rouge on their cheeks. The groups vary from one circle to the next, and each circle has its own leader who sets the pace for the dancing. Off to the side, a foreigner was zealously cranking away at his 8-millimetre camera. As I watch the dances, sadly enough I remember the years during the war. When I was the same age as these young men and women, Japan was already involved in a massive war.

She was there among the spectators. The girl at Swan who had raised her fist as if to threaten her friends. The young woman with slender eyes who grinned foolishly and retained some of the artlessness of a middle-school child in her face, an innocence that made me think of Matryosha, who had been violated by Stavrogin. She wasn't in her uniform today, but wore what appeared to be a hand-knit sweater and carried a muffler.

I observed her painstakingly. Licking her top lip with her tongue, she was entranced by the movements of the bamboo-shoot crew. The look on her face vividly expressed her wish to join one of the circles, but finally the music stopped and the young people took a break. At that moment she looked up and surprise crossed her face when she saw me.

'Hi!' I smiled cordially, as if I had just run into the daughter of a relative. 'Do you live near here?'

'Next to the Odakyū station. And you, Pops?'

Several stands selling fried squid or hamburgers lined the street. I invited her for a cup of coffee, but she kept her hands thrust inside her muffler as she responded that a Coke would be fine. Since it was Sunday, both Yoyogi Park and the NHK plaza were jammed with families who had come out in quest of the sun, so we walked over towards the bench where I had recently sat with my wife. Sitting next to her as I had sat beside my wife, I handed her a bottle of Coke and a bag of popcorn. I had thought her body was childlike when I saw her in her uniform, but studying her now, sheathed in a tight-fitting sweater at close proximity, I could tell, though innocence still lingered in her slit-eyes and protruding eye-tooth, that her bust and thighs had filled out nicely. Examining her tennis-shoes, muddied slightly at the tips, and her sweater, worn from many washings, I tried to imagine a not particularly well-to-do home.

'Do you like them, Pops?'

'Them?'

'You know what I'm talking about. The bamboo-shoot guys. They're just a bunch of country spuds.'

'I like them, though.'

Still clutching her Coke bottle, she turned her body towards me with a scornful look.

'Why're you so interested in those bumpkins?'

'Why . . .? Because I'm interested in young people.'

She said nothing. She peered up at me, trying to discern my true intent. Five or six pigeons had landed nearby and foraged avidly for food, but when a young man wearing a Walkman and a boy on roller-skates with both arms outstretched hurried past, they quickly flew away. We waited until the two young men had moved far into the distance, and suddenly she muttered: 'There's a lot of men like you, Pops.'

'What kind of men?'

'Grown-ups interested in young girls.'

'Are there so many?'

'Lots. When you go walking along Omote Sandō, they call out to you.'

'To you? But those are middle-aged men, aren't they?'

'Some are middle-aged, but there's old men like you, too, Pops.' She grinned, still contemptuously. When she smiled, her teeth showed whitely, like a young girl's. No woman over twenty-five had such teeth. 'Weren't you staring at us in Swan, Pops?'

'What happens after they call out to you?'

'As if you didn't know what men think about.'

'And do you and your friends go along with them?'

'Some do. The old men will sometimes buy you things and give you lots of money.'

'How far will you go if they give you money?'

'To C.'

I asked her what 'C' was, and she told me that most high-school girls called kissing 'A', petting 'B', and going all the way 'C'. I had read of such things in the weekly magazines, but it seemed strangely vivid hearing it directly from this young woman. I stole another glance at her nearly matured body.

'Do you . . . do things . . . like that?'

'No. Not me.'

'What about your friends . . . the ones who come to Swan?'

'They don't either. But I know other girls who'll do it for money.'

I had the feeling this was a lie. Perhaps she was one of the girls who 'did it'. But there was something about her voice that also seemed to be telling the truth.

'You shouldn't do things like that.'

'Uh-huh.' Suddenly she sounded bored. Her tone suggested that it was well past the time for an adult to offer his pat words of advice.

'What's your name?'

'Namiko.'

'Will you be here again next Sunday?'

'I don't know. I might come if I get bored.'

After I got back to my office that day, in my room with closed curtains I tried to work on the draft of my *Life of Jesus*, but my head was filled with thoughts of Namiko and the conversation we had exchanged. I had not, of course, developed any sort of sexual interest in the young woman's body. It was just that I was curious why she should suddenly bring up such a topic with an old man like me – had she been mocking me, had she been trying to give me helpful information, or was she actually trying to seduce me?

Naturally I can't imagine committing an indiscretion with a girl more than forty years my junior. Unlike my youthful days, I had now reached the age when it was too tiresome to upset my personal life, and it was my intention, however imperfectly, to behave like a Christian.

And so, with a certain sense of reassurance, the next day I once again went to Swan to experience my customary pleasure of stealing glances at the young women. To my regret, Namiko and her group were not there. The next day, and the day after, I sat at my usual seat and watched through the window for Namiko and her friends to appear. Four or five days later, when I opened the door of the coffee shop, she and her group were absorbed in conversation. When Namiko saw me she gave no look of recognition, but I felt that was because she was all too aware of my presence. She laughed and frolicked even more gaily than usual.

'She said she'd do anything for a man who'd buy her some nice clothes.'

'She's a fast one, isn't she?'

'Could you go that far?'

Today she was at the centre of the conversation, but I couldn't tell from her tone whether she was serious or not. Perhaps I'm just flattering myself, but I had the impression that she had chosen that topic for my ears. But, according to how you took it, the whole thing might be considered a joke.

'It would depend on the clothes.'

'For me, it'd depend on the guy more than the clothes.'

'If it was a fellow like Michael Jackson, I wouldn't mind cheap clothes.'

'You said it!'

She glanced my way for the first time. She was obviously measuring my response. Then, nonchalantly she proposed: 'Why don't we go watch the bamboo shoots this Sunday?'

'Naw, I hate those country boys. Are you going to go see them, Nami?'

'Yeah, I felt kind of bored last week.'

She didn't look towards me this time. But that, too, seemed like a sort of signal.

On Sunday, I panted my way up the hill leading to the park where the bamboo shoots formed their circles. Since I had a lung removed several years ago, I run out of breath if I don't walk slowly up a slope, and when I suddenly realized that I was racing up the hill panting for breath, I couldn't help but grimace. From the top of the slope the wind delivered the smell of fried squid and the sound of recorded music, and again today a throng had gathered to watch.

I looked for her, but she wasn't there. My feelings of vanity were quashed, and when I realized I had been duped by a girl who could be my youngest daughter, my pride was wounded. *You old bastard.* I heaped insults on myself. *What is it you wanted?* I had no idea myself what I was after.

Still, I thrust my hands into the pockets of my coat and watched absent-mindedly as the young people in Korean-style clothing clasped hands, kicked up their feet, pressed up against one another and twirled around. A dull, unpleasant pain spread through my neuralgic back. As always, the pain made me aware of how old and ugly my body had become, and I watched the bamboo shoots with a sense of envy.

Someone tapped me on the shoulder. When I turned around, she was there grinning.

'I thought you'd be here, Pops!'

'You did?' I started to forget the pain in my back.

We sat on the same bench as the previous Sunday, and I

handed her another bottle of Coke. Just as on the previous Sunday, children wearing roller-skates and young men with their ears plugged by Walkmans scurried around, making me think of the war.

'Do you like music, Pops?'

'Yes.'

'Who do you like?'

'Who? . . . Well, Bach and Mozart and . . .'

'Don't you like pop music?'

I shook my head to indicate that I didn't really understand that sort of music. She looked down, and muttered as if to herself: 'I wish I could just buy all kinds of records. All kinds.'

I studied the healthy swell of her cheeks as she lowered her head. Not a single wrinkle encircled her eyes. Unlike me, this girl still had a long time to live. Her life in the days ahead would open up before her. Compared with that, my life. . . . She dug at the ground with her mud-stained tennis-shoes. As I looked at her shoes, I realized she didn't have enough money to buy a single record.

'There's a Michael Jackson record I want to get, but . . .'

That could have been taken as a request to give her the money for the record.

'Do you really want records that badly?'

'I do! Records and clothes and a Walkman.'

She kept her head down and continued to jab at the ground with the tip of her shoe. Perhaps she had used the same sort of vague hints to lure the middle-aged men who had called out to her. No: maybe this was the first time. Or maybe she was saying it in utter innocence.

'Then, if I buy you a record or some clothes,' I asked jokingly, 'will you do what your friends do?'

She lifted her head and grinned, her eyes narrowing to slits. The simpering smile seemed like an attempt to hide her embarrassment, but likewise seemed like a look of consent; it might even be taken as a sneer at my words. When she smiled, I could see her eye-teeth. It was a smile that knew nothing of life, and simultaneously a grossly obscene smile. The smile, belonging neither to an adult nor a child, disturbed me. Suddenly it occurred to me that a single word from me might be instrumental in determining what became of this girl. 'Then I'll give you the money. In exchange, come out with me twice a month.' A simple statement like that might ultimately cause this girl to lose all faith in men and in love. I, a sixty-year-old man, and a seventeen-year-old high-school girl. She still had a long life ahead of her. I have very little remaining. Yet it would be possible for me to leave the very first fingerprint on this child's life. The sense of pleasure and control was so strong that I impulsively began to say the words to her.

In that moment, the evening sky filled my eyes. The winter sun had just broken through the clouds over Setagaya and Meguro, and that spot alone glittered in the sky. As I watched that glimmer of light, the painting of paradise that had appeared in Stavrogin's dream suddenly manifested itself in front of me. (Beautiful men and women had lived here. They lived each day happy and innocent. The forests echoed with their joyful songs. The sun shed its bright rays on the islands and the sea, beaming down upon its children. It was a remarkable dream . . . the most unlikely illusion that has ever been seen.)

'I've got to go.' I swallowed the words that had started out of my mouth and stood up. When we reached the pavement, we lightly waved our hands to one another as though nothing had happened, and we parted.

Even so, several days later I had the following dream. The location was a hotel room I had used as a workplace many years ago; I had gone into the bathroom and taken off my clothes. My thinning hair, blotchy face and infirm body were reflected in the bathroom mirror. I stood there before the mirror, surprised that my body appeared older than it actually was, and, gripped by a masochistic urge, I stuck out my tongue like a clown at my own reflected face, then laughed aloud. It was no mere laugh; I purposely crowed disconcertingly like a cock.

The dream broke off. When I drifted off to sleep again, this time I was holding down a young woman who protested desperately. The young woman was Namiko. She frantically tossed her head back and forth, trying to avoid my damp lips. The more she tried to get away, the more I wanted to ravage her, and I rubbed my body, the very picture of hideous decrepitude, against her breasts and thighs. I was frantic to sully her eyelids and plump cheeks, where traces of innocence still persisted, with an old man's spittle. This was no act of lust but a literal craving to ravish her very life.

I woke up. Something like smouldering embers continued to glow redly inside my body. I had read somewhere that dreams were expressions of the desires we ourselves do not want to acknowledge, and there was no doubt that the dream I had just experienced was such a dream.

All was quiet, save for the breathing of my wife beside me as she slept. My eyes flashed like a beast in the darkness as I contemplated the dream. My dream had been fashioned by the jealousy that a sixty-year-old man soon to leave the earth felt towards a young woman whose life still stretched before her. It contained the loathing of one whose life withers away towards a high-school girl suffused with life. The pitiful obsession with something I had already lost, and the sadistic impulse to maim a bounteous life, had surely shown themselves like a monster from my unconscious mind and taken that particular shape. A man who had once written *A Life of Jesus* still had such feelings in the depths of his heart.

Close by my wife slept, her breathing peaceful and regular. I thought of the profound difference between her sleep and mine. God grants some a sense of peace as they grow older, while to others He gives a fear of death, a tormenting attachment to life, jealousy towards those who remain alive, and an unsightly, helpless struggle.

Today again I went out for a walk with my wife, who had come to clean my office. It was a warm day, so my back didn't ache, and on the way I even took off the scarf that I had wrapped as a precaution around my neck. My wife was talking about her niece who got married a couple of weeks ago. They had gone to California on their honeymoon.

'Very different from our day, isn't it?'

'It was all we could do to make it to Nara, wasn't it?'

The traffic signal began to change, so we came to a halt, and stood waiting obediently like a pair of love-birds. We were both careful now not to make a run for it, as we had in younger days.

We sat on the bench in the NHK plaza once again. It wasn't Sunday, so we could hear none of the music of the bamboo shoots or the bustle of the crowds. My wife clasped her hands on top of the handbag on her lap.

'It looks like they're going to end up living with his parents. Setsuko doesn't seem very happy about that.'

'That was normal in the old days. It was a real luxury for newly-weds to have a new place of their own.'

This bench is where I sat with Namiko last Sunday. My wife of course knew nothing about that. Just as before, only one corner of the sky glimmered in the sunlight. The painting of paradise that Stavrogin had seen, the kingdom of God that Jesus had described.

'Look. Look, over there where the sun is shining, doesn't it remind you of the way Jerusalem looked from the Mount of Olives?'

'I wonder. The city there seemed whiter.'

As I nodded at my wife's comment, I thought of the manuscript of *A Life of Jesus* that lay on top of my desk. Amidst the crowd mocking the captured Jesus, I locate the figure of one old man. Jesus is meekly led away, covered with grime and blood. He offers no resistance. His eyes are downcast. But when He stands before the old man, He lifts his head. The eyes that gaze on the old man are clear, as clear as the eyes of a young girl. The old man flinches when faced with one whose purity will never diminish. That provokes the old man's envy. Without thinking, he spits upon Jesus. Just as I had done in my dream, attempting to defile at least the physical manifestation of that purity.

A young housewife walked past our bench, and glancing in our direction she gave us a friendly smile. She must have thought that this old couple had finally passed through all the rough seas of life and attained a placid state of existence. And she probably wished she could one day become like that herself.

The Last Supper

'Doctor!'

Mr Tsukada, who was seated next to me in the tiny restaurant, suddenly called out to me. At that, the chef who was brandishing his knife behind the counter raised his head and signalled to me with his eyes. It was a warning not to get mixed up with this fellow, who was well known at the establishment for holding his liquor badly.

Acknowledging the signal, I planted a smile on my face, and in tones intended to deflect the man's overtures to me, I replied: 'What is it?' Then I glanced around the place, preparing to change my seat at a moment's notice should Tsukada start making things uncomfortable for me.

'You're a doctor, aren't you? What the hell kind of doctor?' Though we had only bumped into one another at this restaurant a few times, he didn't hesitate to speak arrogantly to me.

'I'm a psychiatrist.'

'So you take care of neurotic people?' He narrowed his jaundiced eyes and peered into my face. It resembled the dark, sorrowful look that first-time patients give me as they try to appraise me before divulging the torments of their minds.

'But even a psychiatrist knows something about the inside of the body, doesn't he?'

'Well, yes, I had to study that while I was at school.'

'Then let me ask you something. I've had some pain right around here recently. What do you think the problem is?'

Somehow or other, because I'm a doctor, people who know

me sometimes surprise me with questions of this sort even outside the hospital. There is no way I can produce a diagnosis without doing an examination, and, more important, this was the one free day a week when I could slip away from the anguish of my many patients and enjoy a cup of *sake* to myself. As a matter of fact, a look of displeasure darted across my face. But in the same moment, I suddenly remembered the words of Professor Gessel,[1] my academic mentor when I went to Stanford University as a foreign research fellow eight years ago: 'Being a doctor is not a profession. It's a calling, like that of a clergyman, to bear the sorrows of humankind.'

What charming bullshit, Professor Gessel! Muttering to myself, I dropped my voice so that no one else could hear ('No matter who the person is, he wants his illnesses kept a secret' – this was another of Professor Gessel's incessant refrains), and asked: 'Just where does it hurt?'

'Right around here.'

'Is it all right if I press there?'

'Yes, of course.'

The chef glanced quickly in our direction, but was kind enough to pretend not to notice what was going on. I leaned forward, untucked the man's shirt and pressed the area beneath his ribs across to his right abdomen. There I discovered a hard lump.

'Let me see your hands.'

Tsukada thrust his palms towards me like an innocent child. Splotches of redness had spread across the insides of his palms, and his skin was dry and murky.

'Mr Tsukada, have you been to see a doctor at all?'

'Oh no.'

'You have regular check-ups at your company, don't you?'

'They tell me from the X-rays that there's no problems with my chest or my stomach. But after all, this body's been through the war.'

'What about urine or blood tests?'

---

1. In the interest of fidelity to the author's text, the translator has felt impelled to retain all names as they appeared in the original Japanese.–VCG

'That's too much trouble. Doctors in the old days could do their examinations without those kinds of things.'

'They're a lot more accurate. To be frank with you, you ought to give up drinking today. You've done some damage to your liver. Quite a bit, actually.'

In his yellowed eyes flashed a look of dismay, less of distress than that of a child who has had a precious toy snatched from its hand. But I had to intimidate him somehow. A lump on the right side of the abdomen indicated that this fellow was suffering from rather severe cirrhosis. Were he to continue in his present state, obtaining no medical treatment and continuing to drink, he would probably last only another two years.

'Mr Tsukada, please come to my hospital the day after tomorrow. I'll introduce you to the liver specialist in the internal department.'

I pulled out a business card and stuck it in the breast pocket of his jacket. The name of the university hospital where I worked was printed on the card.

'Don't be ridiculous.' He suddenly turned his body away from me. 'You doctors get a real thrill out of treating anyone and everyone like a sicko. When it comes down to it, everyone has a thing or two wrong with them.'

'That's not true, Mr Tsukada.' The chef, maintaining a fake smile, argued on my side. 'Dr Sakai has been saying this out of consideration for you. Why, Mr Tsukada, you're a man of good sense, a company executive, aren't you? You need to take a little care of yourself, and once you're in better shape, then you can start enjoying your liquor again, I'd say.'

'Leave me alone. You're making my *sake* go sour.' Falteringly, Tsukada rose from his chair. A waitress hurried over to support him. 'I'm leaving.'

The other customers watched intently his weary, retreating figure as he staggered out of the restaurant.

With a look of concern, the chef asked: 'Is Mr Tsukada really in such a bad state?'

I nodded. 'I hate to say this, but you mustn't let him drink here any more.'

'He's all but an alcoholic, though,' the chef replied, bewildered.

On Monday, convinced that he would not turn up, I was in the middle of an interview with a female patient I had got to know quite well. Unlike some other psychiatrists, I have studied the methods of the Swiss psychologist, Jung, and so I have my patients describe their dreams. Then I encourage them to create a little miniature garden where I can seek out the unconscious wounds concealed deep within their minds.

This female patient, who was now almost sixty years old, confessed to me that she wanted to divorce the husband she had lived with for many years. Though in their youthful days he had caused her endless torment with his wilful, selfish behaviour, once he had grown old and discovered he had no one else to rely on, he came throwing himself upon her with the full weight of his body, and she could no longer endure his egotism.

Divorce in old age. There was no longer anything unusual about it; it had recently become a common social phenomenon.

I met this woman regularly, listening meticulously to her rancour towards her husband. The simple act of listening was a form of therapy. As I was escorting her from the room, my nurse came in with an uneasy look and reported: 'There's a Mr Tsukada out in the lobby, who says he simply has to see you . . .'

'Really? I'll be right out.' My voice betrayed my excitement. The unpleasantness I had endured two nights before had not been in vain.

When I stepped out into the lobby, Mr Tsukada, like a completely different man, rose respectfully from his seat. He bowed his head and muttered: 'I'm afraid I was . . . very rude to you the other evening.'

'No, not at all. I'm very happy that you've come. I'll arrange things with the internal department at once. Let me get in touch with a doctor I know.'

'All right.' His answer was diffident, and he watched anxiously as I gave instructions to my nurse. Then she took him to the out-patients' receptionist.

As always, having done this much, I felt I had fulfilled my

obligations as a physician. Unlike the situation some years ago, nowadays, even with a life-threatening condition like cirrhosis, a patient who is willing to follow a strict regimen may be able to survive for five or six years. We had to make Mr Tsukada give up alcohol.

The following afternoon, I ran into Dr Kiguchi, the head of internal medicine, just outside the research lab. He was the doctor to whom I had entrusted Tsukada's examination, and he was engaged in a conversation with a young foreign man. This fellow was on the short side for a foreigner, and timid at that, and he spoke to Kiguchi in clumsy Japanese.

When he spotted me, Dr Kiguchi remembered that I had referred Tsukada to him, and he confirmed my fears. 'I haven't seen the test results yet, but your patient is pretty bad. I'm almost surprised he hasn't already developed oesophageal varices and vomited blood. For the time being, I'll try him on Allocain-A and Interferon.'

Then, as though rather embarrassed, he inquired: 'Do you need a volunteer in your department? This foreigner is called Mr Echeñique, and he's come to ask if he could look after some of our patients as a volunteer.'

I smiled bitterly and shook my head.

Evidently Dr Kiguchi had launched into Tsukada quite unsparingly, and when I heard that he was no longer turning up at the restaurant, I felt relieved.

'I wonder why it is, though,' the chef remarked to me when I went to the restaurant after a long absence. 'I feel a bit lonely whenever a customer who really likes his liquor suddenly stops coming altogether.'

'It can't be helped. It's for his health.'

'I know that. To tell the truth, there was something terrible about the way he drank.'

The chef went on to tell me that, compared with his other customers, Tsukada didn't so much drink his liquor as toss it down. He seemed less interested in tasting it than in getting drunk as quickly as he could.

'It was almost like he was drinking because he wanted to forget something painful inside.'

The chef's words stayed with me. Many of my patients tried to camouflage mental torment by drinking. And I remembered the time when Tsukada had got mad at the chef and me, and the desolate spectre of loneliness that had hovered over him as he walked out of the restaurant.

Two weeks passed. That Saturday afternoon, I phoned Kiguchi and went over to the internal wing to find out the results of Tsukada's tests. When I arrived there, Echeñique, the young foreigner I had met earlier, dressed in a white frock-coat, was pushing an elderly man in a wheelchair from an examination-room.

'Well, hello.' I stopped for a moment. 'So you've become a volunteer, have you?' Volunteers were, in fact, not warmly welcomed by our hospital; there were several cases in the past where trouble had occurred between them and some patients.

'Yes, thanks to you.' Answering with dreadful pronunciation, the young foreigner smiled.

Just then Kiguchi, having completed his examination of outpatients, stepped into the lobby, shaking the creosol from his hands.

'The test results are pretty bad, aren't they?'

He sighed. 'He's beginning to show signs of abdominal oedema. I encouraged him to check into the hospital, but he's very unwilling.'

'I see.' After discussing possible treatment of Tsukada, I changed the subject. 'So, I see you've turned that foreigner into a volunteer.'

'Oh, you mean Echeñique? He begged me so relentlessly that I finally asked the head nurse in our ward to take him on. But the nurses seem very happy to have him around. He's very gentle, and he's compassionate towards every patient.'

'He's an odd fellow. Why would he go out of his way to become a volunteer at a Japanese hospital? Do you think he's some sort of fledgling "Amen" priest or minister?'

'No, that's not it. He said he's working here in Tokyo for an

Argentine trading company. That's why he comes on Saturday afternoons, like today.'

In foreign countries many men and women work as volunteers in hospitals, just like common citizens, even if they have no religious calling. Doubtless he was one such individual.

Saturday afternoons are a time when a usually bustling hospital suddenly turns silent. That day, too, not a single person could be seen in the hushed corridors. Then we could hear faint strains from Mozart's Piano Concerto No. 17. It was a piece I had often enjoyed during my study abroad, and now apparently someone from the internal medicine staff was listening to it on the radio during a break.

Kiguchi phoned me at my department.

'It's about Mr Tsukada. It seems he's still drinking.'

'He's drinking?' My brow furrowed of its own accord. For a patient with cirrhosis to be drinking alcohol was equivalent to an act of suicide. That's why both Dr Kiguchi and I had ordered him to stop drinking.

'But. . . .' I started to say something, but I caught myself. My mind had been put at rest when I learned he'd stopped frequenting that one particular restaurant, but that had been careless of me.

'The fact that he can't bring himself to stop drinking,' Kiguchi said with some frustration, 'must mean there's some psychological reason behind it. If that's the case, there's nothing I can do for him as an internist. This is really more up your street. Would you have a look at him?'

As I hung up the receiver, I remembered what the chef had said about Tsukada: 'It was almost like he was drinking because he wanted to forget something painful inside.' But his was no special case: many alcoholics drink every day to dispel the clouds of gloom from their minds.

I had Kiguchi send over the charts, and I focused my inquiry not on his symptoms but on his work, his family situation and his past history. The charts from internal medicine contained sparse information, but I learned that he was born in Kyushu, that currently he was working as comptroller for a company that produces food products, and that he lived alone with his wife. I also discovered that he had two sons who were already married and living on their own. Even such simple information could be of use to a doctor – particularly a doctor who also works in psychological therapy – like myself.

Near noon one day the following week, Tsukada turned up in my examination room on Kiguchi's orders. At a glance I could tell that his face, which had been dark and pale before, was swollen.

'I'm sorry to be causing so much trouble.' The moment he sat down, he placed both hands squarely on his knees and bowed his head. He was a mild-mannered gentleman, the complete opposite of what he became when he was intoxicated.

'Mr Tsukada, are you sure you can't go into the hospital? People who give in to the lure of alcohol when they live at home are really better off in a clinic.' I spoke temperately, trying to show him consideration.

'No. If I'm hospitalized, my illness will just get worse.' He raised his pale, puffy face and shook his head firmly. I sensed sheer determination in the way he shook his head, so without mincing words any longer, I moved to the crux of the matter: 'Is there something in your life that makes it impossible for you not to drink?'

He blinked his eyes and said nothing. His eyes filled with colours murky and sad like the depths of a swamp. For a time he remained silent.

'If there's no special reason . . . won't you tell me what it is that's bothering you? As a psychiatrist and psychotherapist, I would never reveal a patient's secrets to anyone else.'

Once again he resolutely shook his head. 'I can't tell you.'

'Well then, tell me just one thing. You drink because of that agony, don't you?'

He did not reply.

'Please try to relax. I've sat in this room and listened to countless stories of suffering and torment. No matter what you have to say to me . . . I won't be surprised. Having such stories is . . . proof that the person is a human being.'

'No. I can't. No matter what you say, I can't tell you.' Suddenly he grew angry, and in agitation he got up from his chair. 'I'm not coming to this hospital any more.' He spat those words out as if as a reminder to himself and went out of the room. The same shadows of despondent loneliness hovered about his angular back.

Long years of experience, however, left me feeling optimistic. I knew that virtually every patient, like Tsukada, initially rejected the notion of confession. Within their hearts raged a battle between the impulse to divulge their dark secrets and the pain and humiliation of having those secrets known to others. Most likely Tsukada too would spend the next week in the thick of such a battle.

Five days later, my hunch was confirmed. When his weary figure appeared that morning on the threshold of my examination-room, I tried to imagine what kinds of mental clashes he had endured over those days, and on impulse I spoke to him supportively.

'I'm so glad you've come. I've been wanting to see you.'

Once he had settled himself in his chair, Tsukada began to tell me about his sons, to boast about his work and to recall his days of adversity, all the while keeping an eye on my reaction. But he made no move to touch upon the crucial secret.

That didn't matter. As a doctor I knew he was sounding out my responses. After repeating this process many times over, patients would finally strip off their robes of shame and reveal their true feelings to me.

A month of perseverance and patience went by, during which I listened over and over again to Tsukada's boasts and idle chatter. The season had advanced to the green leafiness of early summer, and dull overcast days proceeded one after another. Then, near noon on one such day of sultry heat, Tsukada finally came out with one fragment of his secret.

'I was in Burma during the war. It was dreadful.'

'You mentioned something about that before. Where in Burma did you fight?'

'Along the Nmai Hka River, near the border. Our enemies

were British paratroopers and Gurkha soldiers, and we had almost no ammunition. In any case, we had absolutely no rations left.'

'I understand many contracted fevers, didn't they?' I strained to remember what I had read in some magazine about the pathetic conditions on the Burma battlefront during the Second World War.

'They did indeed,' he muttered as he wiped his face with his hand. 'The field hospital was jammed with malaria patients and the critically wounded. I felt sorry for the soldiers who contracted dysentery. They died in droves every day, shitting in their pants.'

'What about food?'

He suddenly clammed up, as though angered at my question, and peering up at me he said: 'We had none . . . at all.'

'I imagine you didn't.'

'We ate everything that could be eaten. Tree bark, tadpoles . . . even insects we dug out of the ground.' His eyes filled with anger. 'I don't suppose you've ever had an experience like that, have you, doctor? You did stay here in Japan, after all.'

'I went with my parents to a place of refuge away from the city. We didn't have much to eat here in Japan either.'

'You can't compare that to what we went through.' Tsukada's voice rose almost to a roar. I was reminded of the time he had got drunk and picked a quarrel with me. It struck me as odd that he should suddenly become so angry.

Sweat beaded his forehead. Clearly he was grappling with something within his heart.

Suddenly I thought: It won't be long now. Soon he would tell me everything. Hope filled my breast as I gazed at the sweat glimmering on his brow.

In our next interview, Tsukada kept his eyes on the rain trickling down the window as he casually spoke the following words: 'Doctor, at that time in Burma, there were some starving soldiers who ate human flesh.'

I feigned calm, all the while feeling as though a brawny fist had punched me beneath the chin. 'I understand that did happen. I've read that such things occurred in the Philippines and New Guinea too.'

'You're not shocked, doctor?'

'I've heard many more shocking secrets in this room.' Then slowly, in a controlled voice, I played my final card: 'I wouldn't be shocked even if I found out that you had been one of those soldiers, Mr Tsukada.'

'I did nothing like that!' He shook his head violently.

'Isn't it possible, Mr Tsukada,' I proposed, looking into his face, which seemed as dark and terrifying as a swamp, 'that the reason you go on drinking is to forget that agonizing memory?'

Tears welled in his eyes and poured down his lank cheeks all the way to his chin.

'Please tell me. You did, didn't you?'

At my encouragement he nodded, not even troubling to wipe the tears away.

'Whose flesh . . .?'

'Private Minamikawa.'

'Who was Private Minamikawa?'

'Doctor, Minamikawa was my comrade.'

I still remember that day vividly. Outside the examination-room a misty rain fell, sounding like the shifting of sands, while the leaves on the trees had taken on a hue more black than green. And Tsukada, tears pouring from his eyes, related his secret to me in broken fragments. He told me that incessant rains had been falling then in Burma. It was the autumn of 1944, and on high land as marshy as a mudswamp during the rainy season Tsukada's platoon was bombarded by Gurkha and British artillery.

No clear victor emerged in the battle between artillery and machine-guns, so over the space of two days the enemy surrounded the Japanese soldiers who lay prostrate, and the fighting gave way to an exchange of hand-grenades. Their platoon commander was killed. That night, Tsukada's platoon was able to make a narrow escape. They struggled through the marshes, beginning a hellish life on the run as they headed for the Arakan mountain range. Many of the soldiers, no longer able to use their tattered boots, tore strips of cloth from their uniforms and wound them around their feet.

Tsukada and Minamikawa ate everything they could find that was edible. Snakes and lizards were regular fare, and they vied to stuff their mouths with banana stems and worms. With each day the numbers of their comrades shrivelled. Even worse, men who could no longer walk crawled away and hid themselves between the jungle trees, until finally those who could still walk heard behind them the explosion of suicide grenades.

Before long, they realized that some of the soldiers from another platoon who had fallen in with them were hiding something away and eating it. They were told that it was dried lizard meat, but lizards were not that easy to come by, and Tsukada and Minamikawa had a vague notion of what it was. Their nerves had been frayed by the horrors of war, and they feared even to mention openly what they knew it to be.

Although Tsukada's friend Minamikawa had grown feverish from malaria, he exerted all his energy and followed his comrades. Tsukada had got along well with Minamikawa since they had shared the same barracks in the training, and they had survived until this day by helping one another. Minamikawa had left a new bride at home, and the two men were so close that he showed Tsukada his letters from her. And so, for five desperate days, Tsukada had propped up his friend and helped him make it through the jungles and swamps.

When they emerged from the jungle, they encountered the fallen bodies of scores of Japanese soldiers. Some had already died; others looked up at the two men, too weak to rise.

On the seventh night of their flight, Minamikawa painfully told his comrade that he could go no further, and begged Tsukada to go on without him.

'What are you talking about?' Tsukada answered. 'Didn't we promise each other we were going to live and go back to Japan together?'

'I want to go back, but my body can't go any further. Please take care of my family.' Minamikawa wept as he responded.

When Tsukada awoke the next morning, he could not rouse Minamikawa even though he shook him and called out to him. He had died while Tsukada slept.

He wanted to bury his friend, but he had neither the tools nor the strength to dig. Were he to burn the body, there was the possibility that the enemy or guerrilla soldiers might track him down. Tsukada pressed his hands together in prayer, snipped a memorial lock of Minamikawa's hair, and followed the soldiers who continued their retreat.

Tsukada's flight that day took more than its usual toll on his body because of his grief over the loss of his friend. On the second day he fell behind the others and he walked on alone, dragging his legs. By afternoon, unfamiliar soldiers were passing him up in groups of three and four.

'Around nightfall,' Tsukada told me, 'I slipped and tumbled down a cliff. I hit my head and lost consciousness. When I came to, a soldier from another platoon was trying to help me.'

The soldier gave Tsukada some turbid water to drink, then handed him something dark that had been wrapped in paper. It was several blackened chunks of meat. 'It's lizard. Eat it,' the man told him. When Tsukada hesitated, he added forcefully: 'If you don't eat it, you'll die. Think of it as lizard meat, and eat it!'

Tsukada forced one sliver of the meat into his mouth. He closed his eyes and swallowed the morsel.

It was then he realized that the yellow paper surrounding the blackish meat was actually a letter. One glance at the faded handwriting, clearly that of a woman, and Tsukada felt as though he had been pummelled by a fist. It was the same kind of letter Minamikawa had often showed him, and the handwriting was that of Minamikawa's wife.

'Where did you . . . get that meat?'

The man who had fed him gave a devil-may-care laugh. 'Let's see, where was it?' At that, he stood up and was gone.

Tsukada rammed his finger down his throat and vomited. But all that came up was acrid bile. He tried to walk away, but he was unsteady on his feet because of the pain in his legs and hips from the fall.

With the deepening of darkness welled up the fear that he, too, would fall dead to the ground like the many other Japanese soldiers he had seen over many days.

'I stayed there for three days, waiting for my legs and hips to heal,' Tsukada whispered as he stared at the rain through the window. 'There was nothing to eat. . . . So I ended up eating the meat that soldier gave me. . . . It was the flesh of Minamikawa's body. I wanted to live. No matter what, I wanted to live.'

I still remember the soft sound of the rain, the sound that Tsukada and I listened to in silence when he had finished his story.

'When I was shipped back after the war, I thought I ought to take the lock of his hair and visit his home in Uto, but I couldn't bring myself to go. I sent the lock to his wife, and she wrote me back a thank-you note in that same unforgettable handwriting. Then a couple of months later she came to see me, bringing their child along. . . . She thanked me . . . and asked me to tell about his last moments. . . . The child looked at me with eyes that were the very image of Minamikawa. Those eyes were so much like his, I still can't make myself forget them.' Tsukada covered his face with both hands.

'Mr Tsukada. You drink every night to forget those eyes, don't you?'

'Yes. That's right.'

'But not even that child blames you. It's just the way things were.'

Even as I spoke the words of encouragement, I sensed how feeble they sounded. Tsukada could not possibly have been fooled by my remark, a mere pretence at rationalization. When he left my examination-room that day, I could not detect in his retreating form even a trace of the relief that comes from confession. In place of relief, a cloud of loneliness thicker than ever before swirled about him.

The next day, I got a panicked phone call from Kiguchi in internal medicine.

'Mr Tsukada has vomited blood at his house. I think the oesophageal varices have ruptured. . . .'

The worst possible thing that could happen to a patient with cirrhosis had occurred. I tried to picture Tsukada as he vomited up the blood. . . . No, it wasn't the blood in his oesophagus he was trying to disgorge. It was the flesh of his war comrade, the eyes of the child so like his friend's, the memories that had tormented him from forty years ago.

With present medical knowledge, the only viable treatment for oesophageal varices was the kind of surgery performed by Dr S at P University. There were no guarantees that a patient would recover after surgery; normally a considerable amount of danger accompanied the procedure.

Tsukada had the operation and was able to hold on to life for the time being, but his prognosis invited no optimism.

Though his hospital room was outside the jurisdiction of the psychiatric ward, I sometimes dropped in to see him when I had a moment.

Invariably Tsukada's wife, who had shouldered half a life's worth of torment on her husband's behalf, was seated in utter isolation beside his pillow. Occasionally his son would come to see him. Once when I entered his room and he noticed me, a frail smile played on his enervated face, and he muttered: 'Well, doctor, I suppose a man gets what he deserves, doesn't he?'

His remark struck me as an ironic resignation to the fact that the wounds in his heart had not healed even though he had gone through the ordeal of confessing his secret. I was left to feel with some pain the ineffectualness of psychiatry in its attempts to reach into the human heart and soul.

One Saturday, as I got out of the lift, I ran into the foreign volunteer, Echeñique, waiting to get on with Tsukada in a wheelchair.

'OK, we go to examination-room.' Echeñique grinned. 'Mr Tsukada and me good friends.' He pointed to his patient, whose face smiled but looked haggard from his wheelchair. A look at that smile and that gaunt face and I knew that Tsukada's condition was not good, and I could imagine how zealously Echeñique was struggling to help his patient. Even so, I pondered, there certainly are a lot of foreigners who do volunteer work.

The question of why Echeñique came to work as a volunteer every single Saturday when he was also a businessman living in Japan intrigued me. Though I knew it was not that unusual in foreign lands for ordinary citizens to engage in volunteer activities. But how had a foreigner like this been able to unknot a heart tied as stubbornly shut as Tsukada's? And how had he been able to summon forth a pleasant smile on Tsukada's face, the likes of which I had been quite unable to imagine in my examination-room?

Frankly, I couldn't understand it. The whole incident was enough to stir feelings of jealousy in someone like me, who made a living out of probing people's torment. After that I watched with something like amazement whenever the patient went shuffling through the hospital garden accompanied by Echeñique and his wife, or sat in a chair in the waiting-room.

Yet, despite the welcome rejuvenation of Tsukada's heart, according to reports I received from Dr Kiguchi the condition of his oesophageal varices had not necessarily taken a turn for the better.

'There's sometimes blood in his stool,' Kiguchi explained with a measure of perplexity. 'We don't know the reason. We can't work out where he's haemorrhaging from, even when we do an endoscope examination.'

Coming as I did from another field altogether, there was no way that I could help resolve Kiguchi's dilemma. All we could do was watch and wait to see how his condition developed.

And then, a month after Tsukada's hospitalization, what we feared might happen did occur. Once again he suddenly vomited up an enormous quantity of blood.

When Dr Kiguchi notified me, I rushed to Tsukada's room. Several nurses were scurrying back and forth across the narrow private room. An intravenous needle had been stabbed into his arm, and an oxygen tent had been stretched over him. The pallid face of the patient behind that transparent curtain clearly evidenced the severity of the situation.

'How is he doing?' I asked Kiguchi.

'Frankly, tonight will be the critical point. If he survives the night, he'll probably make it another two or three days.'

The stain from a profusion of blood had spread across the floor of the room like a wrinkled map of the world. I could tell immediately from the scope of the stain just how much blood he had disgorged.

The patient waved his hand, labouring to communicate something. When his wife brought her face near his, he clutched her hand and said something to her. She nodded and turned to Dr Kiguchi at the bedside.

'He says he'd like you to call Mr Echeñique.'

Dr Kiguchi looked at me uneasily. The internal department was apprehensive about having a foreigner who was no more than a volunteer come into a hospital room in such circumstances.

'Let's call him.' I thought of how close these two men had grown. One of the nurses placed a call to the trading company where Echeñique worked.

'He says he'll be here immediately.'

After the nurse reported back, we did everything we could to brace Tsukada's physical condition until the foreigner arrived. Though not an internist myself, I had to agree with Dr Kiguchi that it looked unlikely this man would live more than a couple of days.

By the time Echeñique ran breathlessly into the room, Tsukada had stabilized just a bit.

'Mr Tsukada,' he called out. 'Is me, Echeñique. I pray.' That's what I remember him saying. Still in his suit coat, Echeñique knelt down on the blood-stained floor.

And then the conversation between the two men. That night, I jotted down what I remembered of it in my research notebook. I'll copy a portion of it here.

'Mr Echeñique,' Tsukada panted from inside his oxygen tent. 'Mr Echeñique. Does this God you talk about . . . does he really exist?'

'He does. Mr Tsukada, it is true.'

'Mr Eche ñique. I . . . years ago . . . during the war, I did something horrible. Would God really . . . forgive me for that?'

'Is OK, is OK.'

'No matter how . . . horrible?'

'Yes.'

'Mr Eche ñique . . . I . . . during the war. . . .' Tsukada hesitated. Then, in a strained voice he continued: 'In Burma . . . I . . . ate the flesh of a dead comrade. I had nothing else to eat. If I hadn't done that, I couldn't have stayed alive. Someone who has fallen into such depravity . . . could God forgive . . . forgive even that?'

Kiguchi and the nurses stood frozen in utter amazement at the unexpected confession. Only I and his wife had known his secret. I realized that she had known as she muttered: 'Dad, Dad. You've suffered so long, haven't you?'

Eche ñique's body shuddered at Tsukada's words. Still kneeling, Eche ñique covered his face with his hands and did not move. I recalled the shock I had felt when I first heard Tsukada's confession.

But I was wrong to think that Eche ñique shared my initial horror. I must now record the details of my misapprehension. Moreover, I feel it my duty to relate in all seriousness how Eche ñique responded to Tsukada. It is something I must write, not as a physician but as a fellow human being in contemporary society.

'Mr Tsukada.' Eche ñique lowered his hands and straightened his back, and a look of intensity came over his face. He seemed a different person from the clowning, jovial young man who had regularly pushed patients along the corridors in their wheelchairs.

'Mr Tsukada. Do you wish to know? The reason I come to Japan? Do you wish to know?'

Inside the tent, the ailing man nodded feebly.

'Mr Tsukada. I too ate flesh of my friend.'

I still have no idea how to convey the shock that rattled the room at that moment. All I remember is that one of the nurses ran into the corridor and burst into sobs. . . .

'Four years before, while I was college student, I go to visit my uncle in Brazil. On airplane coming back home, the engine goes bad. The pilot was in Andes mountains. The plane, she is broken. Many people are hurt. Andes mountains are very tall. We stay in snow twelve days before people come to help.'

In splintered Japanese, but with intense fervour, Echeñique began to tell his story. And then I remembered reading in the newspaper that an Argentine airliner had crashed in the Andes four years before.

'On fifth day, all food in plane is gone. Everybody has nothing to eat. Every day, some of the hurt people is dying. The person seating by me has hit his chest, and has big injured. . . . This person tells me he is a Father going to Japan.'

I pressed my lips close to the tent and explained to Tsukada that a Father was a Christian priest.

'In the plane this person only drinks liquor. He is drunken man. I could not believe this man is really a Father.'

Echeñique, kneeling there with his back erect. For some reason, as I stared at his slender profile I was reminded of the face of a young farmer painted by Goya. And his confession, because of the stumbling awkwardness of his delivery in contrast to the gravity of its content, seemed more like a recitation of everyday events.

For five days the priest, his chest crushed by his injury and with several ribs broken, managed to stay alive with the help of Echeñique and some of the other passengers. In spite of his agony, he told jokes and tried to keep the other survivors laughing.

'I've been a good-for-nothing drunk of a priest. Next to God, liquor's been the most important thing in my life. After all, being a priest I've got no wife or kids.'

But the day before he died, he said to Echeñique: 'Mr Echeñique, no one has anything to eat, have they?'

Echeñique said nothing, so the priest continued. 'You have to stay alive until help comes. I know I'm going to die. So I want all of you to eat my body. You must eat, whether you want to or not, and wait until you're saved. I know help will come.'

Echeñique wept as he listened to these words. Still breathing painfully, the priest searched for something humorous. 'Fortunately, thanks to the Lord, my body has more flesh on it than the cows at the foot of the Andes. But if you eat too much in one sitting, you'll get drunk. I've got a thirteen-year supply of alcohol inside me.'

He had one additional request for Echeñique. 'When you get out of college, if ever you have a chance to go to Japan, please have a good look around the country I was supposed to go to. I was planning to work at a hospital there.'

The following day the priest died. Echeñique told the other survivors about the Father's dying wish. They consulted amongst themselves, and decided that they would gradually cut pieces of flesh from the bodies of the priest and the other casualties and dry the meat. They were determined to survive by such means until the day of rescue.

'I too eat.' Echeñique closed his eyes and muttered. 'But then I eat also his love. As I eat, I think that I will find a job with a company that has work in Japan, and on my vacation time, I will be volunteer at a hospital.'

The faltering Japanese came to an end. It was silent inside the tent. Tears slowly coursed down Tsukada's sunken cheeks. I watched as Echeñique thrust his hand into the tent, and as Tsukada's bony fingers returned the grip as though desperately searching for something. It was at this point that the nurse ran from the room and burst into tears.

'It's been a year since Mr Tsukada died, hasn't it?' the chef asked me. I was sitting at a small table at the far end of the counter, drinking and watching the TV news.

'Huh. Has it been a year?'

'I can still remember his stooped shoulders, when he'd stagger drunk out of here. He was a nasty drunk, but now that he's dead, I kind of miss seeing him.'

'Every person has a different story to tell about their lives.'

Yesterday, and again the day before, I listened to patient after patient relate the torments of their hearts. Mothers betrayed by their sons, daughters-in-law debilitated in both body and soul because of doddery parents. Wives who have ceased to love their husbands, husbands abandoned by their wives. Echeñique has been transferred to Osaka, and he is doing volunteer work at a Christian-run hospital there.

On the television, the newscaster was reporting the events of the day.

'A former university student, who was convicted of shooting to death a female classmate in Paris and then eating her flesh, returned to Japan today. . . .'

A Woman Called Shizu

One evening, as the autumn rain was falling, I set out for the Shimbashi Playhouse. I was going to see *Singing Is My Life*, a play featuring Fujita Makoto and Sakai Wakako.

I had known Mr Fujita for some time, and twice when my novels were made into films or television plays, he had taken the lead roles. He had even made a recording of a song I wrote in jest.

I had known of Sakai Wakako since her rise to popularity, and I had always been fond of her reserved personality, so unlike other contemporary actresses.

These were the reasons why I had wanted to see this well-reviewed play featuring the two performers. For many days running, the playhouse had been sold out to various groups, but thanks to Miss Sakai I was able to obtain a seat in the very front row.

Singing Is My Life was a play depicting the life of the late popular singer, Shōji Tarō. He was a figure far removed from the young fans of today who go into frenzies over pop singers like Matsuda Seiko and Kyon-kyon, but some may remember him as the white-haired elderly singer who stood tall and un-bending on such television programmes as *Songs from the Good Old Days*. In this play, Mr Fujita portrayed every segment of Shōji's career, including of course his years as a popular singer, and even his pathetic days after the war when he lost his fans and had to wander on the road from one provincial theatre to another.

That rainy autumn day, every seat in the playhouse, from the ground floor to the third balcony, was filled.

The curtain rose. The first scene opened around 1930, when Shōji Tarō, then working in Dalian, Manchuria, for the South Manchurian Railway Company, formed a mixed chorus of young workers in the company. The woman who assisted him and accompanied the chorus on piano was the woman who would later become his second wife, Watanabe Shizu.

At the time, Shōji Tarō was married and had two sons, but his relationship with his wife, Hisae, soured around the time he decided to quit his job, which he had reluctantly taken on orders from his parents, so that he could make an attempt to become a singer. Eventually they were divorced.

Afterwards, he fell in love with Watanabe Shizu, who had quietly shown her understanding of his decision, and the two were married. That was the story covered in the first half of Act One.

As I sat in the front-row seat and peered up at the stage, my neck began to hurt. On top of that, the man to my left kept pressing obnoxiously against my arm with his right elbow, and though I glared at him from time to time, as if to say 'This is my territory, pal', he ignored me. While my attention was caught up in this confrontation, the second scene began, in which the feelings of Watanabe Shizu, played by Sakai Wakako, start to bend towards Shōji Tarō. As I looked up at the stage and glared at this man, glared at the man and looked up at the stage, my admiration for the play-writing skills of Umebayashi Kikuo mounted to the point that I forgot all about the man in the next seat.

During the years of 1930 and 1931, which were being played out on the stage, I was an elementary-school student also living in Dalian. Because of a work assignment my father, a bank employee, had brought his family to live in this Manchurian city when I was about four years old.

Winters in Dalian were icy. And interminable. I walked to my school, which was in the centre of town, and on the way home from school I always made at least two detours with friends.

First we would slip into the head office of the Southern Man-churian Railway, where we sidled up to the steam and warmed our tiny, frozen bodies. My friends and I were all dressed in small overcoats and gloves and even scarves around our ears, but when we dived into buildings from the outside, we always felt as if we had been saved. Standing next to the steam we would watch with curiosity as the adults worked busily, and sometimes, carrying documents back and forth, they would call out: 'Boys! On your way home from school?'

When we had half warmed ourselves in this manner, I would part here from my friends and climb the hill that was my second major hurdle. Although it was still only two or three o'clock in the afternoon, the hill was frozen solid, and very often I would slip and fall. So this hill leading towards my home was frighten-ing and I hated it. . . .

Once I reached the crest of the hill, panting as if I had been mountain-climbing, I still didn't go straight home, but instead passed through the gate of a quiet neighbourhood house. Snow was still on the ground, and the door was tightly shut, but on the wall there was a doorbell, which I still remember being slightly yellowed. I also have the distinct impression that a bare acacia tree stood to one side of the entrance.

Invariably a dog would start barking inside the house. I waited patiently for the dog's owner to open the door from inside.

When the door opened, I was greeted by a warm stove, and by a woman with a rather swarthy complexion but beautiful eyes. I called her Auntie.

'Did you fall down again?'

'Yes.'

'You're hungry, aren't you?'

'Yes.'

She made me wash my hands, then fed me fruit and biscuits. This particular brand of biscuits can no longer be found in confectionery shops, but they were in the shape of the Western alphabet – A, B, C – or took the form of dolls and horses.

She lived alone in the house. I was young at the time, and I no longer remember how many rooms she had besides the one where she kept the piano. I gave some of my biscuits to her shepherd dog, which she kept inside the house. Auntie left me to do whatever I wanted, but I was never bored. The shepherd dog, for all his enormous size, was gentle and played with me.

'Why do you keep your dog inside?' I once asked her. I was curious, because my mother had scolded me for picking up a stray and hiding it in my room.

'Because I'm all alone here.'

'Why are you all alone?'

'Because I haven't got married yet.'

'Why haven't you got married?'

She smiled with a tinge of sadness in her face. I can still summon up images of that wry, bewildered face from a layer of my memory.

Near dusk, I would get tired of playing with the dog and announce: 'Well, I'm going now.'

'All right.' She would nod, turning towards her make-up mirror and running her hands lightly through her hair. 'I have to lock the door, so go on out ahead.'

'All right.'

The perceptive dog, perhaps realizing he was going to be left alone, would coil around her and bark. Auntie would rebuke the dog, then lock the door and meet me outside the gate, where we began to walk through cold so piercing that it hurt your ears.

This time I would not fall or slip on the frozen snow. She held tightly to my hand.

Next to my mother, I loved this woman best, and I was delighted on those occasions when she came to our house for a visit and ate dinner with our family.

She and my mother were devoted friends. They had not met here in Dalian, but in fact had gone to school together.

My mother attended what is now called the University of the Arts; at that time it had been called the Ueno School of Music, and she studied the violin there. Auntie graduated from the same course a little behind my mother.

My mother got married and moved to Dalian because of her husband's work, but I never found out why Auntie had come to Manchuria. And being an elementary-school student, I had no interest in the reason either.

But even a child in those times could sense that war would soon come to Dalian. Outside our house at night I could hear the creak of boots crunching the frozen snow as soldiers wearing winter uniforms and shouldering rifles marched past. It was a portent that the times were slipping towards a dark pit.

Whenever Auntie came over to our house, she and my mother studied music together. Sometimes she played the violin while my mother accompanied, but usually she played the piano for my mother. When they had finished, my brother and I would plead with them until they joined us in a game of cards.

It's pathetic to have to say this myself, but in those days I was a lot more dim-witted than my brother, and I could never win at any kind of competition. When I played Old Maid with Auntie and defeat was at the door, she always let me win by purposely drawing the Old Maid card herself, but I didn't have a clue that was what she was doing until my brother later told me, so I'd say to her: 'You're really bad at this, aren't you?'

Oh, and then the following also happened. Once when my mother was ill, Auntie attended a parents' association meeting in Mother's place. The teacher wrote in large letters with chalk on the blackboard:

> COLD
>
> LAUGH
>
> FUN

Then the teacher, dressed in a black uniform with a closed collar, ordered the students: 'Write the opposites of these words.'

Parents and brothers of the students were lined up at the back of the room. Most of them were mothers, and they all smiled as they proudly watched their children diligently writing words on their papers. I was conscious that Auntie was there in place of my mother, standing in a formal kimono and wearing a serious expression on her face.

Convinced that the opposite of 'COLD' was 'DLOC', I wrote 'DLOC' on my paper. I put down 'HGUAL' as the opposite of 'LAUGH'. Stupidly, I was persuaded that 'opposite' meant to read the words backwards.

'Now, show us your answers.'

I handed my paper in to the teacher along with everyone else, then sought out Auntie with my eyes and grinned at her. It was a signal that I had got them all correct.

The upshot hardly needs to be mentioned. With a grimace, the teacher read aloud my answers and those of one other student, sending the mothers into gales of laughter.

'It's all right. Don't worry about it.' Auntie tried to buck me up as we walked home. 'Everyone makes mistakes like that when they're young. Even I did.'

When we got back to my house, my mother talked to her briefly, then tried to cheer me up by saying: 'You're not like your brother; you're a late bloomer. Listen, a "late bloomer" means someone who becomes better the older they get. Your brother has good grades now, but you have the ability to become outstanding later on.'

Auntie nodded broadly. 'That's right. She's quite right.'

The next afternoon, as I went out ice skating with a friend in the neighbourhood, I announced: 'They say I'm a "late bloomer".'

My friend Yokomizo, the son of the owner of the confectioner's, sniffed and said: 'Wow.' Like me, he had no idea what the term meant. Perhaps he thought it was something like measles or whooping cough.

At a place called Mirror Pond where the children went to skate, we met up with a number of others we knew. As I was changing into my skating boots, I declared to the group: 'They tell me I have great bloomers!' At some point, 'late bloomer' had been transformed in my head to 'great bloomers'.

'Wow,' they all answered. I doubt they had any idea what I was talking about either.

When winter came to an end and the ice on Mirror Pond melted away, the many spiraea in Dalian hesitantly began to send forth buds. During the spring in southern Manchuria, the flowers all gush forth at once like a spray of water. Come May, flower petals from the acacia trees dance on the wind throughout the town.

Even as a child, I felt joy in the flowers of spring. As my mother and I walked along the path in the park festooned with pure-white flowers, she taught me the song 'The Orange Trees Have Blossomed' and I felt happy. Mother taught me a series of songs about Manchuria written by the poet Kitahara Hakushū, and I made up my own nonsense versions:

> Mother bought me ten caramels;
> I ate three
> And gave one to Spot.

One afternoon when I rang the doorbell at the entrance, the shepherd dog barked as always. It was not, however, a menacing bark, but a bark of joy that his friend had come to see him. While I played with the dog, Auntie leaned against the window-sill and stared at the springtime sky. Soft, cotton-like clouds floated in the sky.

'What are you looking at?' I asked.

'Japan.'

'Japan?'

Having moved to Dalian as a young child, I had virtually no idea what kind of place Japan was. Left to my own imaginings, I concluded from reading my school textbooks that Japan was a beautiful, dreamlike country.

'That's right, Japan. One of these days a good friend of mine is coming from Japan.'

'A good friend?'

'Yes. . . . A good friend of Auntie's.'

Her back still towards me, she stared at the springtime clouds. I didn't even know whether Japan was in that particular direction. From behind, Auntie seemed to be taking pleasure in her thoughts . . . to me, she looked as happy as I felt.

On the stage of the Shimbashi Playhouse the story of Shōji Tarō's days in Dalian raced to a swift conclusion. Amidst the flurry of activity, Watanabe Shizu's heart gradually inclined in his direction, and the playwright adroitly implied that, as catastrophe loomed for Tarō in his marriage because of his wife's lack of understanding, his love for Shizu grew.

During the thirty-minute intermission after Act One, a man from the Shōchiku production company took me backstage so that I could deliver a box of chocolates and pay my respects to Sakai Wakako, who played the part of Shizu. Cloaked in a dressing-gown, Wakako poured both of her visitors a cup of black tea.

Even as I joked with her and got her to laugh, in my mind I was still reflecting on the cruel winters and flower-strewn springs in Dalian. The little house that stood atop the slope of frozen snow. The barking of her shepherd dog, and the back view of Auntie as she leaned against the window, waiting for someone to come from Japan. . . .

That had all happened so long ago. Now I have grown old and have passed through a wealth of experiences in my life. And there was life in Auntie that spring day. As an elementary-school student, I had merely been too young then to realize it.

Late in the autumn of that year, as the age itself grew dark, a grey cloud began to form over my family. For reasons which neither my brother nor I could comprehend, the relationship between my mother and father suddenly ruptured. Every night we could hear them arguing in the parlour. Stretched out prone on our beds, my brother and I would lift our heads from the juvenile magazines and comic books we were reading and listen intently to their voices. 'Go to sleep!' my brother angrily shouted at me. He wanted to hide his feelings of anxiety from me.

Sometimes when I returned from school, Mother would be by herself in the chilly room, wiping away tears. Sometimes she sat there rigid as a stone statue. Occasionally she would be talking about something with Auntie. When I came into the room, the two of them would paste on smiles and ask: 'How was school today?' But the tear stains on Mother's cheeks didn't escape me. I did my best not to look at her, averting my eyes and clowning and joking, pretending that I had seen nothing.

With each passing day, the demeanour of my parents made it evident that their relationship was drawing nearer to the point of catastrophe. When we ate dinner together at night, Father scowled and Mother stared down, wordlessly fiddling with her chopsticks. I would steal glances at their faces with fear in my eyes.

By this time, Auntie almost never stayed to eat dinner with us.

I began to avoid going to her house to play. I still wanted to visit her, but I didn't want her to know about the heartache submerged deep inside me. I grew lonely at school as well. My classmates would have been unable to understand the loneliness I felt as a child. Come Monday morning, they would gleefully discuss the hiking excursion they had taken with their parents the previous day.

'We went to Jinzhou! There's a river there filled with killifish.'

Until just a year before, my parents had often taken my brother and me hiking. On our way home, I had always been the most exhausted, and the first to fall asleep in the *mache* horse carriage. Father scolded me for that every time.

I hid away within my heart the sorrow that I could reveal to none of my friends or teachers, and I wandered the streets here and there until nightfall. Going home and seeing my lonely mother sitting in the dark room, not even bothering to turn on the lights, was just too painful for me.

I would watch half-heartedly as two or three *mache* drivers got together and played a game like chess beneath the leafless acacia trees, or delay my return home by scribbling graffiti along brick walls. As my house drew near, I would detour to a side-road and walk far off into the distance.

One day as I was wandering about, my knapsack slapping against my back, I was tramping down a street far from my home when a woman's voice called to me from behind.

It was Auntie.

'What are you doing here at this time of night? Aren't you going home?'

I looked up at her face without saying a word. She seemed to understand from the expression in my eyes.

'Let's go to my house. I know the dog'll be happy to see you.'

I yielded to her suggestion and went to her house for the first time in many months. I heard her dog barking at the entrance.

She poured me some black tea and fed me some Russian cakes that were sold at Naniwa-chō.

'Let's get you home. I'll go with you.'

I walked alongside Auntie down the streets which were already fogging over with evening haze. The bare acacia trees towered blackly in the mist, and from time to time *maches* passed by, their wheels creaking. Another winter was rapidly approaching.

'It will be all right. I know it will.' Suddenly she clutched my hand very tightly. 'You don't need to worry. I know everything will turn out all right.'

I still said nothing. The urge to weep assaulted me, but I withstood it with all my might.

That was the first memory of 'separation' I had ever encountered in my life. Since that time, through the simple process of living, I have experienced any number of painful separations with other people, but this was my first bitter parting.

'I don't even appear in the second act,' Sakai Wakako commented, drawing the collar of her dressing-gown together. The colours of her gown had faded a bit, suggesting she had worn it for many years.

'What about the third act?'

'That's the scene where Shizu falls ill and dies. I just lie there in bed without any lines to say. I was really surprised how hard it is just to lie still.'

'I imagine it is.'

With curiosity I looked around the actress's dressing-room. When a performer acquires the stature of someone like Miss Sakai, the corners of her dressing-room are piled high with gifts of flowers, and even a refrigerator is provided. Three long, white, cushion-like objects hung from her costume-rack. These, she told me, were breast and buttocks pads worn with a kimono.

When a young female assistant and the wig dresser came in, we hurriedly got up and left the dressing-room.

After the second act, which depicted Shōji Tarō during the war, singing on behalf of wounded soldiers, the third act presented the lonely life of this singer following the war, when he had lost all his fans. Once the top star in the world of song, Tarō was dislodged by younger singers, and after wandering through the provinces for some time, he ended up undergoing cancer surgery. The person who encouraged, comforted and brought strength to him in his late years was his wife, Shizu.

From those scenes, in which I think snatches of actual conversations must have been employed, I learned for the first time how Mrs Shōji – the woman I had called Auntie in my childhood – had spent the last years of her life.

Finally exhausted, perhaps, because of the care she had to give her husband, she herself fell ill. Her condition did not improve, and she grew progressively weaker. On the day she died, Tarō came rushing back from his performances on the road and rubbed his wife's feet. I shed unexpected tears at that scene.

So that's how she died, I thought.

Sakai Wakako's portrayal of the final moments of 'Auntie' thrust a knife into my memories. I had known nothing of the latter half of her life. I had been aware of nothing but her brief period of happiness in Dalian.

As I stared at the stage, I compared her with my mother.

In those days. . . .

Auntie had lived all alone, waiting for Shōji Tarō to return from Japan. But she had in no sense been lonely.

'One of these days a good friend of mine is coming from Japan.' She had muttered the words as she leaned against the window-sill and stared at the cotton clouds. Happiness and joy had radiated from her profile.

Beside her I visualized my mother, whose marriage had fallen apart in the foreign city of Dalian. The lonelier she became, the darker her face grew, so unlike that of Auntie, who still brimmed with hope.

Up on the stage, invisible to any of the other spectators, and seen only by me, another woman made her entrance from the wings. It was my mother. Two women, both of whom had studied violin at the Ueno School of Music, and both of whom had lived for a time in Dalian. I watched their divergent lives played out on the stage.

The play ended at 8.30. I walked out to the street amidst the theatre groups, hailed a taxi and returned to my office in Harajuku.

I turned on the lights in my office, glanced over at the photograph of my mother in her later years that was propped on my bookcase, and opened up a book in an effort to drive it from my mind.

Ah, yes. Two more things I must add.

Actually, I once met Shōji Tarō towards the end of his life.

It was some sort of party. I can't for the life of me remember what kind of party. (Maybe it wasn't even a party, but some sort of small gathering, anyway.)

That was the first time I had met him, of course. He didn't know me, but I recognized him instantly from his tall, thin body and his distinctive hair-style and black clothing. He sat by himself in a corner chair. There seemed to be few people chatting with him.

Midway through the party I went over to introduce myself to him. Though I was considerably younger than he was, Mr Shōji assumed his rigid posture and bowed his head deeply in greeting. When I told him I had spent my youth in Dalian, and that Auntie Watanabe had treated me with great affection, a look of surprise crossed his face.

'She had a shepherd dog.'

'Yes, she did! So you really knew her, did you?'

'Yes.'

For a few moments Shōji was silent, but suddenly a look of indescribable sadness floated in his eyes behind his round-rimmed glasses, and he blurted out: 'Shizu was . . . to me she was . . . a goddess.'

I learned from the newspapers that he died about a year after that.

In the spring four years ago, a writer friend of mine called Agawa Hiroyuki and I boarded the *QE2* from Hong Kong and sailed to Lüda, formerly known as Dalian. This was my first visit to Dalian since the fifth grade, when my parents had already divorced and my mother took me and my brother back to Japan. Because Agawa's father had been forced to work in Manchuria, he had visited Dalian two or three times during his school-days.

I felt as though I had been whisked back to my childhood in a time tunnel. The shape of the city, the streets and roads, the rows of acacia trees planted at regular intervals along the road-side, the houses – everything was as it had been in the past, nothing had changed . . . except that everything was older, had fallen into decay, had become dirty. And the plazas and buildings that had looked so broad and tall to me as a child all seemed to have shrunk in size and scale.

We visited the old house where Agawa's sister had lived, then went searching for the house where I had grown up as a child. When I got out of the car, familiar roads, familiar buildings and the acacia trees that I had used instead of bases to play baseball darted one after another before my eyes. Running my hand along the wall and stroking the trunk of our acacia, I stood before my old house. Our interpreter remarked that, owing to the housing crunch, three or four families lived in each house. All the pleasant and painful recollections from my childhood welled up in my breast, and I could scarcely bring myself to leave, but I couldn't keep Agawa waiting, so I returned to the car.

'Where would you like to go next?'

Agawa, who fancies anything that could be called a vehicle, asked to see the railway station.

The car travelled slowly along several streets, then started down a slope. And suddenly I remembered, that Auntie's house had been at the top of this slope. I looked back. The house had already retreated into the distance, yet cotton-like clouds marking the onset of spring floated above the hill.

But the house was already far behind us.

'What are you looking at?' Agawa asked.

'Nothing,' I answered. 'Nothing at all.'

The Box

I have placed several pots of *bonsai* trees and plants in my Harajuku office, so that they can provide a little warmth to my heart when I take a break from work. I call them *bonsai*, but they're really nothing so grand. I've just lined up a few cheap potted plants that I have bought every year at the plant market as I've strolled of an evening beside Shinobazu Pond at Ueno, in search of some relief from the stifling heat of summer.

When I sleep over in my office, the first thing I always do, after waking up in the morning and washing my face, is feed some seed and greens to the tiny birds I keep. Then it's my habit to give the plants some water. But last summer, a female editor who had come to my office on business, told me: 'Did you know that when you're watering your plants, if you talk to them they can understand you? You probably think that's non-sense, but give it a try.' A gentle-hearted, married woman brought up in the downtown *shitamachi* district of Tokyo, she is very fond of plants.

To be frank, I was sceptical about her remarks. I thought it was ridiculous, but at the same time I felt there was a chance that plants had some kind of special faculty, so that even if they could not understand human speech, they might be sensitive to the wishes we expressed for them.

At the time, I had just planted some morning-glory seeds in a pot. I've been fond of morning glories since my childhood, and I wanted to be able to see their large blossoms each morning in the corner of my stifling office.

At the beginning of the day after the editor suggested it to me, each time I watered the morning glories I said to them: 'Please have lots of flowers.' But I realized how insinuating and self-seeking my voice must have seemed to the flowers, so the next time I took a deep breath and spoke to them in all earnest.

My one-sided entreaties continued day after day. As if my petitions had been granted, that summer the single pot of morning glories produced a mass of coiling buds which started turning the colour of strawberry ices, and two or three days later when I opened my eyes in the morning, I was greeted by beaming flowers.

If that had been the end of it, I should have thought nothing out of the ordinary had occurred. But when summer drew to a close, I began to speak differently to the morning glories.

'Don't wither up on me. Keep on blooming.' With these words of encouragement, I poured water on them.

As a result, to my surprise the morning glories kept producing flowers into the autumn. Of course it wasn't one or two a day like it had been in the summer, but at least two blossoms a week delighted my eyes.

'Take a look at this morning glory,' I boasted to the house-keeper. 'It seems to understand human speech.'

'It's true,' she responded. 'This is the first time I've seen morning glories blooming in November.'

'All right, then, since this really works, I'm going to make them bloom during the winter too!'

I doubt anyone will believe what I'm going to say next, but I have a photograph of myself holding a pot with large blooming flowers while snow is falling outside. It's quite true. The photograph that proves it all, a noteworthy photograph that ought to be published in the *Guinness Book of Records*, is pasted in my photo album.

It was the day after a heavy snow had fallen in Tokyo. Despite the weather outside, in my office the large, red morning glories seemed to be spreading their arms proudly. I asked my housekeeper to take a photograph, and I went and stood outside my apartment building with the pot in my arms.

Passers-by stared at me wide-eyed. I said nothing, but I was filled with pride.

Exactly what is it I want to say, starting with such an anecdote?

What I'm trying to express is the fact that humans and animals are not the only ones who have hearts and language and faculties. Things we tend to think of as simple objects – even stones or sticks – have some kind of power living inside them. That's what I'm trying to say.

This happened ten years ago.

Towards the end of summer, I was puttering through a village in Shinshū in a car. In a small cottage in a place called Naka Karuizawa I had been working on a rather long novel, and in late summer, as all the summer villa owners were finally taking their leave, I had somehow finished off the novel, and had decided that I wanted to travel the old highways through Komoro and Ueda and Saku that still retained the smells of the Shinano region.

I had been to Komoro and Ueda many times over, and when I stopped the car I took on the look of a man who knows his way around, peering into old temples and sliding open the soiled glass door of an antique shop I stumbled across.

In a hushed afternoon back-street in Ueda, I found a tottering antique shop that also dealt in used furniture. When I opened the badly hung door, to the left stood a bureau-shaped medicine cabinet that doctors in the old days had used, while pot-hooks hung down from the ceiling, and at the foot of the stairs rustic-looking saucers and a wash-basin had been piled up. The prices of such items have escalated markedly in Tokyo antique shops recently, but ten years ago out in the countryside they were sold at such cheap prices that no one gave them a second glance.

An old woman was leaning against a rectangular *hibachi*, reading a newspaper.

I picked through several objects, until finally my eyes lighted on one. 'What's this?' It was a commonplace box, nothing more than a wooden box wrapped in brightly coloured paper. But inside was a stack of pamphlets, their inks faded from exposure to the sunlight. There were hymn collections and pamphlets from a Protestant church, and children's stories about Jesus. It even contained an old Bible. When I flipped through the Bible, several picture postcards fell from between its foxed pages. The sentences on the postcards had been written in foreign characters. The reverse sides were decorated with photographs of foreign cities and drawings of Santa Claus. A volume resembling a photo album was buried beneath all these items.

Unrelated to my profession as a writer, I am a man of ardent curiosity. I pulled out the faded album and began leafing through it because the worms of curiosity began squirming inside me. But, for some reason, only three photographs were pasted inside the album. There were obvious signs that seven or eight other photographs had been torn out.

'Excuse me, ma'am,' I called out to the woman by the *hibachi*. 'Is this box for sale?'

'Which box is that?' She slowly got to her feet and walked over near me. 'Oh, that. Well, yes, it's for sale, but there's not much point in buying a lot of rubbish like that.'

'That's true. It can't be called antique, after all.'

'I imagine he must have brought it along with some other things from a foreigner's house in Karuizawa. My husband, you see . . .'

'Your husband?'

'After the war ended, they sold off furniture and wall clocks from the foreigners' villas. He probably brought this along with some of the other things.'

'How much do you want for it?'

The old woman peered at me, then answered pityingly: 'Something like this, yes, you can have it for nothing. It's just junk.'

'I couldn't do that.'

I don't remember how much I ended up giving her. I doubt if I parted with more than around 500 yen. She thanked me over and over again, but her eyes made it clear she regarded me as a fool for buying something like this box.

I paid money for what was obviously rubbish because of the old Bible, and because one of the three photographs pasted in the album depicted the old highway through Karuizawa during the war.

It sounds a bit quaint to talk about 'the old highway', but today it's become the main street of Karuizawa, and come summer both sides of the road are jammed like chocolate boxes with branch outlets of Tokyo shops. Along this road bustling throngs of young people, each looking the same and each dressed in the same styles, scurry back and forth.

But the old Karuizawa highway in that photograph appeared to be a scene from either before or during the war. The vista it presented was dark and forlorn and gloomy, like a film set after shooting has been concluded. I remember that scene, however, because I came to Karuizawa once or twice during the war. For that reason, I did not feel that I had lost anything by buying the wooden box decorated with brightly coloured paper, both as a token of the past and as an object of curiosity.

In the dining-room of my cottage that evening, I positioned a small electric stove next to me (when it rains in Karuizawa, even at the end of summer, it turns quite chilly inside my mountain cottage) and began looking through the photographs on the postcards and the horizontal characters scrawled on them.

Fortunately for me, a number of the postcards were written in English and French, which I could read, while the remainder were in incomprehensible German. From the addresses, I was able to determine that the postcards had been sent to a woman with the French-sounding name of 'Mademoiselle Henriette Lougert'. Though the name sounds French, one cannot say with any certainty that this woman was French herself. There could be Belgians with such a name, and it is possible that a woman from Canada could have the name as well. In any case, convincing myself on my own authority that the statute of limitations had already passed, I haltingly began to read the words on the postcards.

They all seemed to have been written by her friends and acquaintances, and the contents asked for news about or inquired after the health of her father, who was also living in Japan; a husband and wife wrote that they were in Madrid, but that an infant delivered by their friend, Madame Blange, had died; another complained that life in Rome had grown exceedingly difficult. One declared that its author was absorbed in reading Tolstoy and Turgenev, and described what the children were doing. There was even a postcard that asked, half-jokingly, whether Japan was really like the country that appears in *Madame Butterfly*.

Sliding my feet closer to the electric heater, then pulling them away again, I wondered what kind of woman this Henriette Lougert had been. It occurred to me that she might have been the wife of a Protestant minister. I had heard before that a number of missionaries from Canada had come to Karuizawa in the old days to escape the summer heat. I even had the impression that there had been a teacher of that name at the Athénée Français at Ochanomizu, which I had attended five or six times and then left many years ago.

In addition to the photograph of the old highway, the album contained a picture of some foreign women carrying parasols as they picked flowers – there were two or three Japanese children with them – and a photograph of the railway station on the Kusakaru line that had once stood below the old highway. Each picture was yellowed and faded, and filled me only with a sense of the passage of time. I imagined that the foreigners and Japanese who appeared in these photographs were all dead by now. Such depressing thoughts must be the result of my advanced age.

Several days later, I removed the photographs from the album and strolled down the old highway, which was still alive with festive activity even though the end of summer was at hand. From time to time I pulled out a dim photograph and compared it with my surroundings, alternatingly experiencing surprise then delight at how much the same scene had changed over the years.

Now I remember. As you climbed the old highway, there had once been an old hotel, the Tsuruya, which was frequented by such writers as Hori Tatsuo, and on a back-street nearby had stood a laundry. I remembered that the owner of the laundry was a man who knew all there was to know about wartime Karuizawa. *I ought to ask that old man.*

I passed by any number of shops that were plastered with signs reading BARGAIN or DISCOUNT, jostling again and again against crowds of young people dressed in tennis outfits and slurping soft ice-cream, until I finally reached the cleaners called Tsuchiya. Regrettably, the owner was out on business. I showed his wife the photographs and asked if she knew any of the people in them.

She shook her head. 'My family's from Iwamurata. I don't know anything about what this place was like during the war. When my husband gets back, I'll get him to phone you.'

I left the photographs with her, and by the time I got back to my cottage in Naka Karuizawa, the phone was already ringing.

'I'm sorry. I was out on some business.'

'I told your wife what this is all about. Do you happen to know the foreigners in the pictures?'

'It's Mademoiselle Louge. I knew her.'

The laundryman called Mademoiselle Lougert 'Mademoiselle Louge', which I suppose is what the locals in Karuizawa must have called her.

'She lived up by Mt Atago . . . the villa is still there. A Japanese bought it after the war, though.'

Mt Atago stands at the rear of the old highway. A friend lived there one summer, but he complained that the humidity was tremendous. But because it's Karuizawa, summer homes have been built up there for many years.

'But sir, how did you end up with a photo of Mademoiselle Louge?'

'I just ran across it in an antique shop in Ueda.'

'In Ueda, eh?' For some reason, the laundryman went silent for a moment. I sensed that there was something to his silence. Call it a writer's intuition, which is unusually accurate. The story which follows is a summary of what the laundryman hesitantly told me the following day, after I brought him a bottle of whisky and we sat down to drink it.

A dark, gloomy, at times even dismal atmosphere hung over Karuizawa during the war, an atmosphere that young people today could not begin to imagine. The atmosphere resulted from the fact that foreigners from various nations, on the pretext that they were being evacuated from military targets, were assembled here, and while on the surface they led normal lives, in reality they were under surveillance by the Japanese secret police and the military police.

Also, in the beginning, they were provided with special rations that were better than the food the Japanese were eating, but eventually, once everything grew scarce, they could not even lay their hands on black-market rice or potatoes, since they had no connections in the provinces, and they began to suffer from malnutrition. They started to roam about the villages near Karuizawa, begging people to sell them eggs or milk.

Mademoiselle Louge (though 'Lougert' is the correct pronunciation) was the daughter of a minister who had come to Japan to proselytize, and each summer for years they had come to Karuizawa to escape the heat. When Mademoiselle Louge was nineteen, her Japanese mother died of tuberculosis, and thereafter she worked as a typist at an embassy in Tokyo while she looked after her ageing father. When the war turned fierce, the Japanese government advised all foreigners to return to their homelands, but her father, who was a citizen of a neutral nation, applied for and received permission to live in Japan because of his illness.

When bombing raids on Tokyo became an almost daily occurrence, the embassy where Mademoiselle Louge worked took refuge in Karuizawa. She took her infirm, elderly father and moved into their mountain cottage near Mt Atago.

Having come here every summer since her childhood, she knew the people of the town well. As a result, she was able to obtain food initially without much difficulty.

Once the villagers began to run short of foodstuffs themselves, however, they stopped sharing rice and potatoes with Mademoiselle Louge and her father. Crop yields were anything but abundant in this tranquil, impoverished region.

It was not unusual in those days to see foreigners set out on bicycles, knapsacks hanging from their backs, to try to buy food as far away as Furuyado and Oiwake. Mademoiselle Louge was one of their number. But neither the peasants of Furuyado nor of Oiwake had sufficient rice or wheat to share with outsiders.

When bombs began to fall on Tokyo, some people burned out of their homes fled on foot to the Karuizawa area. These people begged food from the farmhouses they passed along the way, but once that became an everyday occurrence, the villagers began refusing, and one night in the ice-house, the cellar where ice cut in the winter was stored, a man was found dead with straw crammed into his mouth.

In these circumstances, the foreigners too shed all their pride and pleaded like beggars for food, but the villagers could only shake their heads.

It was during such times that Mademoiselle Louge met a young Japanese man. In a settlement at some remove from Karuizawa she wandered from house to house seeking milk and potatoes for her father, and at each house she was refused. Just then, a young man on a bicycle happened along. The artless young man had close-cropped hair and wore work clothes, and when he heard Mademoiselle Louge's story, he went to talk to the master of the farmhouse from which she had just been turned away. When he returned, the young man reported: 'He's says they'll give you just a little.'

What he sold her, however, could hardly be called ' a little', for she left with her knapsack stuffed with potatoes. Moreover, the young man generously strapped the knapsack on to his bicycle-rack and went with her as far as the railway station.

'Every once in a while, I can bring you over some potatoes. Please give me your address,' the young man said curtly as the whistle of a train sounded far off in the mountains. 'I sometimes have work in Karuizawa.'

He said he worked in the district post office. When Mademoiselle Louge asked why he had not been enlisted in the army, he told her he had been drafted but was sent home the very same day because of pleurisy. Then he divulged that his health had improved and he was waiting to be inducted a second time.

These were times when it was dangerous to rely upon the kindness and the words of others, but Mademoiselle Louge had the distinct feeling that this young man actually would come to Karuizawa with food for her. There had been that much of the country boy's earnestness in his face.

When two weeks, then three weeks passed with no sign of him, however, Mademoiselle Louge abandoned hope.

It was late that autumn when the young man turned up, on a cold day of gloomy, incessant rain. He brought the promised potatoes, as well as apples and a bottle of goat's milk. When Mademoiselle Louge returned from the embassy, her father was sitting in his rocking-chair and, to her surprise, sitting beside him was the young man, snapping dried twigs and stoking the fire in the stove. Because her feeble father could not do any physical work, the young man had asked if there were any chores he could do until Mademoiselle Louge came home from work, and so he had been cutting firewood and chopping logs with an axe.

He joined them for an evening meal of steamed potatoes. The Louges had nothing else to offer him but some jasmine tea from Hong Kong.

After the young man had gone home in the rain, her father smiled and said: 'That Japanese fellow is a good boy.'

'He really is,' Mademoiselle Louge replied.

Thereafter, as though his first visit had been the turning-point, the young man came often. And he always brought something in secret. Once he even brought a can of marinated beef that was impossible to obtain.

'This stuff is hard to come by,' he said responding to her look of amazement. 'A relative gave it to me.' He would add nothing to that clipped explanation. How kind he is, Mademoiselle

Louge thought. In gratitude she wrapped a book in paper and gave it to him, saying: 'Here is some nourishment for your heart. You have given my father and me nourishment for our bodies. In return, I give you nourishment for your heart.'

The heart nourishment was a Bible. Mademoiselle Louge's father was a minister, and she shared the same faith, so she hoped more than anything that this pure young man could also come to know the teachings of God.

The young man accepted the book and thumbed through it. 'I'll try reading it,' he said, putting it into the bag that hung from his shoulder.

She was gripped by a desire, like that of an elder sister or a mother's love, to apply even more polish to this simple, honest young man's character.

'Umm . . . we have to do this very quietly, since the police are troublesome, but on Christmas Eve my father and I and some friends are getting together at the church on the old highway. We'll be offering prayers there. Would you like to come, Mr Fujikawa?'

Fujikawa was the young man's name. His face stiffened for a moment when she asked the question, but he answered: 'At night?'

'Ah, I suppose it's too far to come from your village.'

'Well . . . could I bring a friend?'

'Of course you can. Is it a female friend?'

'No,' he blushed. 'A man.'

Mademoiselle Louge was confident in her heart that a friend of Fujikawa's could be trusted.

On Christmas Eve, some fourteen or fifteen of the foreigners who had been evacuated to Karuizawa assembled at the church. There was no sign of Fujikawa or his friend, so around 8 p.m. they began their prayers, and from his chair Mademoiselle Louge's father related the story of the birth of Jesus.

Midway through the story, Mademoiselle Louge noticed Fujikawa and a rustic-looking, middle-aged man peering at them through the window of the church.

She was thrilled, convinced that God had given them a

wonderful Christmas present. Beaming, she brought the two men into the church, and once her father's recitation was concluded, she introduced them to her friends. The middle-aged man bowed his head deeply to the foreigners, and seemed in all respects to be filled with gratitude. Prayers were resumed, and after the Christmas observance the group chatted together until nearly midnight over home-made bread and the choicest black tea they had been able to find. Mademoiselle Louge and some other foreigners who could speak Japanese interpreted for the two men, and they seemed to have quite an enjoyable time. When they stole quietly outside, the chill of the night air was extreme, but the stars glimmered brightly and all befitted the image of the holy night.

The next day, as Mademoiselle Louge was about to set out for the embassy-in-exile where she worked as a typist, a man she had never seen before was waiting for her in the roadway.

'You are Miss Louge?'

'Yes.'

'I'm from the military police. We'd like to talk to you, so please come with me.'

The tone of his voice made it clear she had no choice. As she stood there in astonishment and fear, he stepped up beside her and led her down the frozen road in the direction of the old highway.

The office of the military police in those days stood right next to the Karuizawa railway station, and sometimes they would interrogate suspicious-looking visitors as soon as they stepped off the train. Mademoiselle Louge was not taken to that office, but instead to a villa surrounded by a spacious yard and set apart from the neighbouring houses.

She was placed in a room with no furnishings other than an unlit stove, a crude table and two chairs. There was no decoration of any kind, and the bare walls were covered with stains. Outside the window she could see the wintry forest, its trees stripped of their leaves. Finally she heard footsteps and the door opened, and in came the middle-aged man, Ono, who had accompanied Fujikawa to the church the previous night. His timid, obsequious behaviour from the night before had vanished, and he seated himself in one of the chairs, spreading his legs arrogantly. Fujikawa stood behind him.

'In terms of nationality,' Ono said with a smile, 'you are a foreigner, but your mother was Japanese. Do you consider yourself a Japanese while you're here, or a foreigner?' Once he had extracted from a cowering Mademoiselle Louge an oath that she had not forgotten her identity as a Japanese, he suddenly spoke to her gently: 'Well, then, do you think we could get you to do something for Japan?'

Throughout the interrogation, Fujikawa stood at the back, his honest-looking face tightly constricted.

The help they wanted was for Mademoiselle Louge to inform them of the sources of telephone calls and mail coming into the embassy where she was employed.

'What do you think? Does that sound distasteful to you?' Ono mumbled as he drummed on the table with his index finger. In the forest outside the window, a wild bird shrieked.

Though Mademoiselle Louge could have known nothing about it, a secret peace initiative was being advanced under the leadership of statesmen from a faction opposed to Prime Minister Tōjō Hideki who had left Tokyo and come to Karuizawa to escape the air raids. A plan had been advanced among their ranks to request that the neutral nation which had hired Mademoiselle Louge serve as intermediary for their peace proposal. The secret police were naturally keeping a close eye on the group's movements.

Fearfully, Mademoiselle Louge shook her head. Her beliefs would not sanction such a contemptible act.

'So, you don't like the idea? That creates some difficulties.' Ono stretched his words out slowly. 'Then shall I turn you over to Fujikawa?' He rose from his chair. 'Don't feel you must hold back because she's a woman.' With that, he disappeared.

'Take my advice. Please co-operate with us.' Fujikawa spoke pleadingly. 'If you don't, I'll have to hurt you. Your father may also be harmed. What we're asking you is very important for Japan's war effort.'

Mademoiselle Louge began to shake when she thought of her old, frail father being tortured.

'Please don't do this. I beg you.'

'It can't be helped. I don't want to do this myself, but orders are orders.'

'I . . . I can't do it. I'm too frightened.'

'Don't worry about it. All you have to do is make sure they don't discover you.'

At that moment, Ono came back into the room.

'What's the verdict, Fujikawa? Has she agreed?'

'No, but I think she will soon.'

Ono seized Mademoiselle Louge's hair and slammed her head into the table.

'Your boss was at that gathering last night, wasn't he?' He ground her face into the table with even greater force. 'You're not dealing with children here!'

'What if we gave her a day to think it over?' Fujikawa tossed her a lifeline from the side. It was their technique to trade off between a whip and a lollipop.

She was released for that day. But the following day a man was waiting for her on the frozen road. Thinking of her elderly father, she had no other choice. She agreed to co-operate.

Fortunately for Mademoiselle Louge, none of the kind of phone calls the police were expecting came in to the embassy, and not a single letter from a Japanese that could be construed to touch on the peace initiative arrived in the mail. At first Ono suspected that she was hiding information, but when Fujikawa dressed up as a plumber hired to repair some frozen sewer pipes and searched the embassy, he could find no signs of a conspiracy either.

Most likely, the people involved in the peace initiative had guessed what the military police were up to and had been careful not to blunder.

At the end of his story, I asked the laundryman how he had learned of these events.

'Well, you see, I had a cousin who was in the police then. He told me about it after the war.'

The story was not all that surprising to me. In gathering material for stories, I had heard even more frightening accounts of the activities of the military police in Karuizawa. I have written about such events elsewhere, and even used them in altered form in my play, *The Rose Palace*.

But the laundryman's story was not finished.

'About a year after the war ended, Mademoiselle Louge's father died, but she didn't go back to Tokyo. She stayed in Atago. She continued with her typing, and taught foreign languages to the young ladies, and she worked for the church as well.'

Then one day an American jeep carrying MPs came from Nagano in search of Mademoiselle Louge. This was perhaps six months after her father's death. At the time, Tokyo and virtually every other part of Japan had been reduced to scorched earth, and the people were about to face their second autumn of starvation and cold. Concurrently, individuals who had co-operated in the military effort and committed war crimes were being interrogated and put on trial, one after another. She was placed in the jeep and taken to Nagano city. There she was questioned by a US military interrogator about her activities during the war. She was asked whether she had been subjected to torture by the military police.

Mademoiselle Louge shook her head. The lieutenant who was examining her looked at her peculiarly and asked: 'Are you sure?'

'I am sure,' she answered.

'Then you don't know these men?' He had an MP open the door. From the shadows of the doorway stepped Fujikawa and Ono, their faces gaunt, dressed in US Army fatigues. 'Are you sure these men did nothing to you?'

At that moment, Mademoiselle Louge recalled with stark clarity how, on that winter morning, these men had clutched at her hair, rammed her head into the table, and threatened and intimidated her. An unspeakable anger swept through her breast.

'They did nothing to you?'

'I remember these men,' Mademoiselle Louge answered. 'These men . . . I. . . .' She paused. 'They gave me and my father potatoes. They brought us goat's milk. We were starving then.'

An interpreter translated precisely Mademoiselle Louge's reply for Fujikawa and Ono. With lowered eyes they listened to the unexpected words.

'I heard that, much later on, one of the two men went and visited Mademoiselle Louge in a Tokyo hospital. I suppose he must have gone to say thank you. She had contracted cancer and didn't have much time left. I feel sorry about that.'

At the height of the war, I had stayed for a couple of weeks in a hamlet called Furuyado near Naka Karuizawa. I was a college student, and I remember one foreign woman who came to the farmhouse where I was staying and asked in broken Japanese if she could buy some eggs. Mademoiselle Louge had been one of those foreign women evacuated to Karuizawa.

I left the laundry and headed for the bus-stop, walking along an alleyway behind the old highway. Young men and women were riding around the back-street on rented bicycles and taking photographs of one another.

I returned to my cottage and had another look through the materials in the box. As I glanced absent-mindedly at the postcards addressed to Mademoiselle Louge – actually, to Mademoiselle Lougert – I suddenly noticed something strange. Various names were written in as senders of the postcards, but their addresses were peculiar. One was from a certain number in Luke Avenue in Rome. Another was from an address in Matthew Street in Madrid. Luke and Matthew are, of course, names of two of the four Gospels in the Bible. In fact, all of the addresses on the postcards had the names of one of the Gospels.

I stared at them for some time. Then, struck by a thought, I pulled out the old Bible from the wooden box. It was musty, and its pages had turned brown from the humidity.

With a postcard return address of '10–5 Viale S. Luca, Rome', I turned to the fifth verse of the tenth chapter of Luke. There it was written: 'And into whatsoever house ye enter, first say, Peace be to this house.' The message on the card said: 'The baby at Madame Blange's house has died of diphtheria. It is very sad. But Madame has recovered emotionally.'

I caught my breath. This may be just arbitrary speculation on my part, but I began to wonder if this was not an allusion to the fact that peace negotiations had broken down.

The next postcard was addressed from '27–1 Calle S. Mateo, Madrid' and contained the message: 'Recently I've been reading Tolstoy and Turgenev.' I knew without even opening the Bible that the first verse of the twenty-seventh chapter of Matthew's gospel described the convening of a meeting by the Sadducees to discuss whether Jesus ought to be killed. Tolstoy and Turgenev were, of course, Russian authors. Linking these two ideas, I thought of the Yalta Summit where the United States, Great Britain and the Soviet Union met to discuss the conclusion of the war.

There was, of course, no proof for any of this. It could be nothing more than my imagination. But wasn't it possible that friends of Mademoiselle Louge who had already returned to their homelands were conveying news of the war situation as they understood it to Mademoiselle Louge and her father in this fashion? And . . . and perhaps she had placed these postcards in her Bible, which she would leave on the prayer altar of the church. Someone would open it up, and pass the news to someone else.

I grew excited. But it was an unfounded excitement, perhaps nothing more than a phantom. And yet, had Mademoiselle Louge hoped that, after her death, this Bible and these postcards would pass into the hands of someone like me? I couldn't help but feel that, in fact, these several postcards, filled with the truth of the matter, had taken on a will of their own, and had been waiting patiently inside the wooden box for many years until they could be read by someone like me.

Perhaps I think up such nonsensical, irrational things because I am getting old. That's why I speak to every one of the potted plants in my office each morning. I think plants must converse with each other, and I have the impression that trees and rocks and even postcards saturated with the thoughts of men must all speak to one another in hushed voices.

Afterword

Once he reaches a certain stage in his career, a writer little by little learns to understand the literary themes that have absorbed him throughout his life, as well as the strengths and weaknesses of his technique. At the same time, he gradually comes to discover if his own talents lie in the short story, in the novella or in the novel form.

In my own case, I have found that the best way to give concrete embodiment to my themes is to continue alternating between the writing of short stories and novels. Still, a good deal of time passes between the point when I drive the chisel into the block of ice and the moment when I can first sense that my characters have begun to move.

When those characters begin to move, I write a short story about them in a different locale. This allows me to breathe a fuller life into them. As a result, I can only assume that the characters who appear in the short stories collected here must be living in some form or other in the longer works I am composing even now.

Over the years I have forged intimate familial ties with these characters, who reflect portions of myself. Consequently, even a character who appeared only once in a short story waits in the wings, concealed by a curtain, for his or her next appearance on stage. Not one of them has ever broken free of his familial ties with me and disappeared forever—at least, not within the confines of my own heart.

Shusaku Endo